"A provocative sight—the moon and you!"

Sean's American drawl startled Sarika, and she spun around. "Are you trying to tempt me, Sarika?"

"I wouldn't want to tempt you if you were the last man on earth!" She bit out the words, her heart pounding wildly. "You're not my type."

That was the wrong thing to say—she knew it instantly!

"What kind of man is your type, then?" He laughed softly, but it was not a pleasant laugh and she leaned back against the pillar, away from him. "The type you can pick up when you're interested and drop the minute you're bored?"

"Most certainly not!" she gasped indignantly. "I have no interest in men!"

"You make that sound like a challenge, Sarika," Sean said as he leaned toward her. "And I've always been a sucker for challenges!"

Books by Yvonne Whittal

HARLEQUIN ROMANCE

2002—THE SLENDER THREAD
2077—DEVIL'S GATEWAY
2101—WHERE SEAGULLS CRY
2128—PRICE OF HAPPINESS
2162—HANDFUL OF STARDUST
2198—SCARS OF YESTERDAY
2243—MAGIC OF THE BOABAB
2249—LOVE IS ETERNAL
2304—BITTER ENCHANTMENT
2358—THE MAN FROM AMAZIBU BAY
2412—SUMMER OF THE WEEPING RAIN
2430—SEASON OF SHADOWS
2441—THE LIGHT WITHIN
2478—THE SPOTTED PLUME
2538—HOUSE OF MIRRORS
2616—RIDE THE WIND
2742—WILD JASMINE

HARLEQUIN PRESENTS

498—THE LION OF LA ROCHE
550—DANCE OF THE SNAKE
558—BITTER-SWEET WATERS
574—LATE HARVEST
582—WEB OF SILK
590—CHAINS OF GOLD
598—THE SILVER FALCON
630—DARK HERITAGE
726—WHERE TWO WAYS MEET
782—THE DEVIL'S PAWN
790—CAPE OF MISFORTUNE

Wild Jasmine

Yvonne Whittal

Harlequin Books

TORONTO • NEW YORK • LONDON
AMSTERDAM • PARIS • SYDNEY • HAMBURG
STOCKHOLM • ATHENS • TOKYO • MILAN

Original hardcover edition published in 1985
by Mills & Boon Limited

ISBN 0-373-02742-7

Harlequin Romance first edition January 1986

GEETA HARIBHAI
who laid the foundation
on which I could build this book,
and I could not have done so
without her invaluable assistance and guidance.

Printed in U.S.A.

CHAPTER ONE

THE departure lounge at Heathrow Airport was almost filled to capacity with people of all races and nationalities waiting for their flights to be called. Sarika Maynesfield spotted an empty seat and walked towards it with a fluid, natural grace that drew several appreciative glances, but she was unaware of the interest she aroused. She was tall and slender, with hair the colour of wild honey hanging in a thick silken mass down to between her shoulder blades. Tawny, almond-shaped eyes were veiled mysteriously beneath long, dark lashes, and there was an added touch of mystery in the faint smile curving the full, sensitive mouth beneath her small, straight nose. Her suit was a rich, creamy colour cut in a fashionable style, and it was set off by an olive-green blouse with a wide embroidered collar. Sarika's femininity was unquestionable, and so was her beauty, but it had been a liability rather than an asset while she had studied for her degree in architecture.

She sat down between two travel-weary female tourists and carefully crossed one long, shapely leg over the other before opening the magazine she had bought at the bookstall. She stared down at the glossy pages advertising the latest fashions and found herself thinking of the two weeks she had spent in Paris with Jane Summers. Jane was studying fashion designing, so it was only natural that they should have visited most of the fashion houses in Paris, but there had also been time to take in the architectural beauty of the city. At the end of their two weeks in Paris Jane had gone farther south, to Cannes to join her parents, and Sarika had had to return to England alone.

Her lovely mouth drooped slightly at the corners. She was thinking about the graduation ceremony three days ago, and her ultimate disappointment when she discovered that her parents would not be able to attend it, but now at last she was going home, and this time it was not merely for a holiday. *Home.* The word echoed through her mind and aroused a mixture of feelings. Home was in Bombay on the west coast of India and, after the freezing winter she had endured in England, she looked forward to India's warm, sultry climate.

Sarika's mind cruelly conjured up her last holiday in Bombay. Gary Rowan's handsome, laughing features intruded between her and the printed pages of the magazine she was paging through, but she firmly thrust aside his image as well as the painful memories it aroused. She had to think pleasant thoughts. She was going home to her parents, and to a possible future in her father's architectural firm. That was what her father wanted, that was what she had studied for, but the idea did not appeal to her. Her thoughts once again took a definite swing towards the unpleasant, and this time she could not halt them. She had wanted to start a little business of her own, a boutique specialising in traditional Indian saris, but her tentative plans had been doomed to a quick death when she had approached her father on the subject. He had refused her the financial support she had required for the initial layout of this private venture, and the ensuing argument had not succeeded in changing his mind.

'I refuse to throw good money away, Sarika,' he had declared with a flat finality. 'I've seen to it that you have everything you need, and more. I've encouraged you to travel the world during your holidays, and I've paid a fortune for your studies, but I refuse to waste money on this ridiculous idea of yours. You're going to be an architect, and your place is with me in the company.'

Dave Maynesfield had spoken the cold, harsh truth. She had always had everything his money could buy for her, but what neither he nor her mother had known was that Sarika had craved their love and attention a great deal more . . . *that*, and the opportunity to stand on her own two feet. Her father's money had opened doors for her, but emotionally she had always been like a starved child standing outside a cake shop with her nose pressed to the window. Dave and Cara Maynesfield had mostly been too busy living their own lives. Their social activities had taken them all over the place, and no function, apparently, was a success without them.

'British Airways flight number zero-zero-three will now depart for Bombay. Will all passengers please proceed through gate number six.'

The announcement came as a welcome relief from her depressing thoughts, and Sarika picked up her hand luggage and slipped the strap of her sling bag over her shoulder as she rose and walked towards the departure gate where a queue was rapidly forming. It was five in the afternoon, London time, and she would not arrive in Bombay before six-thirty the following morning. She knew from experience that it would be a long, tiring flight, and she was not looking forward to it.

The passengers were attended to swiftly and, when Sarika's boarding pass had been checked by the ground hostess, she followed the elderly Indian couple ahead of her towards the chute that gave access to the Boeing parked on the tarmac. The flight hostess smiled at her with recognition when she boarded the aircraft, and she was shown to her seat in the first class section. Sarika disposed of her hand luggage, and sat down, her fingers automatically searching for the seat-belt and fastening it about her. She could feel the engines vibrating beneath her, and it heightened the excitement of going home.

The man who sat down beside her was possibly in his early thirties, and his briefcase indicated that he was travelling on business. Sarika paid little attention to him. She was looking out of the window at the lights of the airport building. It was raining; it had been raining for days, and she shivered almost as if the cold and the damp had penetrated through the walls of the Boeing.

It took some minutes before the passengers were all seated, then the Boeing began to move from the position where it had been parked. It turned, and taxied slowly towards the runway, and while this was happening the flight hostesses were instructing the passengers what to do in case of an emergency. Sarika was barely listening, she had heard it all before so many times, and at long last the Boeing was prepared for take-off. The engines were revved, the Boeing began to speed along the runway, and then they were airborne.

Sarika leaned back in her seat with her eyes closed. The sensation of flying through the air in that enormous silver machine never failed to instil a certain amount of awe and fear, and she had no idea how long she had sat like that when a familiar voice roused her.

'A glass of wine, Miss Maynesfield?'

'Yes, please,' she replied to the hostess's query and, when the glass was placed in her hand, she murmured her thanks absently.

Sarika sipped her wine slowly, and gradually began to relax. In the process she also released her mind from bondage, and allowed her thoughts to wander almost at will. It was eight months since the last time she had been home, and she realised now how much she had actually missed it, but the reason for her long absence away from Bombay did not bear thinking about at that moment.

Bombay was home to Sarika. Her parents had left England twenty-five years ago to settle in India, and two years later Sarika was born. Her father had wanted a son, and Sarika had never been allowed to forget this. Her mother, tall, sophisticated and beautiful, had never hidden the fact that motherhood had not been her forte, and she had willingly left Sarika in the capable hands of Ayah, the Indian woman, whose duties had been swiftly changed from housekeeper to nanny. There had been no other children, the decision had apparently been mutual between her parents, and Sarika had grown up alone and embittered despite her father's wealth.

Ayah had been more than a nanny. She had taken the place of a mother and a friend, and she had showered Sarika with love and affection, but it had never entirely compensated for the parental love Sarika lacked. It was also Ayah who, knowing of her parents' love for India, had suggested the name 'Sarika', and Dave and Cara Maynesfield had agreed to it.

She was jarred back to the present when the hostess leaned over her to snap the adjustable table into position. Her dinner was placed in front of her on a tray, and Sarika smiled her thanks. She stared at the contents of the tray. It looked tasty, but it was nevertheless plastic food, and for some unaccountable reason she thought of the old-fashioned, spicy mince pie Ayah always prepared for her. It was her favourite, and the mere thought of it made her mouth water, but instead she had to be satisfied with boiled meat and vegetables, fruit salad, and biscuits and cheese.

'Why do young women always worry about their figures?' a male voice enquired beside her, and Sarika realised that she must have been staring at her food in a way that made him suspect she was thinking of her figure. 'My name is Bruce Watson,' he smiled at her. 'What's yours?'

'Sarika Maynesfield,' she reciprocated, aware of his appreciative glance sliding over her speculatively, but she was not unduly disturbed by it.

'Sarika?' he frowned. 'That's an unusual name.'

'It's of Hindu origin,' she answered abruptly, and he looked taken aback.

'Does it have a special meaning?'

'It means "equal to everyone",' she explained coolly, removing the cellophane wrappers from the neatly packaged food.

'Equal to everyone?' Bruce Watson laughed. 'That sounds like a Women's Lib slogan!'

Accustomed to remarks of a similiar nature, Sarika had a cutting reply handy. 'It takes a chauvinistic male to recognise it.'

'Touché!' he grinned, attacking his food and leaving her to sample her own, but he did not leave her in peace for long. 'Are you going to Bombay on a holiday?'

She shook her head and swallowed down a mouthful of food. 'My parents have lived there since before my birth, and I'm going home to join my father's company.'

'As a typist?'

'As an architect,' she corrected with dignity, and a certain amount of pride.

'An architect?' He studied her with renewed interest. 'I would never have guessed.'

'Because I'm a woman?' she asked, the light of battle instantly flickering in her eyes. 'Do you think women are incapable of competing with men in that field?'

'You misunderstand me,' Bruce Watson laughed good-naturedly. 'If I'd been asked to guess your occupation I would have said you're a fashion model. It's the way you move and the way you dress, perhaps, but it just proves how wrong one can be.'

Sarika accepted that in silence and concentrated on her dinner. They talked for a while longer when their trays were removed and their coffee was served, but she was soon bored with his obvious interest in her, and she picked up her magazine to discourage further conversation. Bruce Watson was perceptive enough to get the unspoken message and, after ordering himself another drink, he lifted his briefcase on to his knees and took out a wad of official-looking documents which he began to study intently.

Sarika did not read for very long. She was, in fact, not taking in a word of what she had read anyway. She was tired after the hectic two weeks in Paris with Jane, and then there had been the lengthy, tension-packed graduation ceremony she had had to attend. She covered her legs with the small blanket which had been provided and lowered the back rest of her seat, but she could not sleep. Her thoughts went rushing back into the past, and this time she could not thrust Gary Rowan so easily from her mind.

There had been several men in her life for brief periods of time, but she had known from the start that although they found her pleasant and attractive company, their main interest had been her father's wealth. Gary Rowan had been different . . . or so she had imagined. She had believed that he cared for her, that his protectiveness and concern for her was genuine, and during their whirlwind courtship she had allowed herself to fall in love for the first time in her life. She had trusted him, and she would have defended him with her life if necessary. That was why, when she discovered the truth about him, it was a crippling blow from which she knew she would never recover entirely.

Sarika tried to curb her thoughts, but they raced on like a wild horse which had broken its tether. She could recall every sordid detail as if it had happened the day before, and her mind gave her no peace as it replayed the incidents like an old movie.

She had been dining out with Gary at a popular restaurant frequented by the young people in Bombay. They had danced, and she had perhaps had too much wine with her dinner. Or perhaps it had simply been her happy state of mind which had made her feel light-headed when she eventually excused herself and went to the ladies' room. Two girls in the adjoining cubicles were engaged in a conversation, but Sarika had paid little attention to what they were saying until Gary's name was mentioned. Frozen, and incredulous with shock, she realised that they had been discussing her relationship with Gary, and they had gone into detail about the things he had told them of his relationship with her. It had been the easiest thing on earth to get her to fall in love with him, Gary had apparently told them. He had actually found Sarika inhibited sexually and quite a bore, but she was putty in his hands, and, if everything went according to plan, the Maynesfield millions would soon be his. They had laughed about it as if it was a hilarious joke, but Sarika, sensitive to the extreme, had been crushed and wounded so deeply that she doubted if the scars would ever heal.

The humiliation of what had occurred still clung to her like a second skin, and she groaned inwardly as she emerged from that red mist of pain and remembered suffering. She could feel the beads of perspiration on her forehead and tight upper lip, and she made a near physical effort to thrust the hateful memories from her.

If only she could relax and sleep. The lights in the Boeing had been dimmed, and Bruce Watson appeared to be dozing in his seat beside her, but sleep continued to evade Sarika. It was some time before she succeeded in clearing her mind sufficiently, and only then did she sink into a fitful sleep from which she awakened periodically to ease the stiffness in her limbs.

The grey dawn sky filtered in through the window beside her when she got up to stretch her legs, and she went to freshen up in the compact cloakroom of the Boeing before returning to her seat. After the long flight she felt stiff and tired, but her physical discomfort took second place to the excitement of seeing her parents and Ayah again. Oh, how she had missed Ayah!

Breakfast was served, but Sarika was barely conscious of what she was eating. Bruce Watson was talking to her, but she was not listening. The early morning sun was almost blinding as it glittered on the Adriatic Sea far below them, and when the breakfast trays were removed, Sarika sat with her eyes glued to the window for her first glimpse of the Indian coast.

She did not have long to wait. In the distance land was clearly visible, and it was excitingly familiar to her.

'Good morning, ladies and gentlemen,' the air hostess's voice came over the speakers in that calm, toneless manner which was intended to soothe. 'We are approaching Bombay airport and will be touching down in approximately ten minutes. Please fasten your seat belts and adjust your seats to the upright position. When the "No Smoking" light comes on please extinguish your cigarettes, and we trust that you had a pleasant flight. Thank you.'

The Boeing was losing altitude when Sarika snapped her seat belt into position. Bruce Watson smiled at her. It was a smile that said: 'We're almost there', and she was so delighted at the thought that she actually smiled back at him with more warmth than she had intended. She glanced out of the window again, and Bombay's harbour came into sight as the Boeing dropped lower and reduced speed. It would not be long now before she would step down on to familiar soil.

The last few minutes to touch-down seemed to drag interminably, and then there was the slow taxiing of the aircraft as it left the runway to approach the airport building. It stopped at last, and the weary passengers seemed to have new life injected into them as they collected their hand luggage and walked along the aisle towards the exit.

Sarika was burning with impatience, and after what seemed like yet another eternity she stepped out of the Boeing and into the brilliant morning sunshine which blinded her momentarily. Oh, how good it was to feel the heat of it against her skin!

'Perhaps we'll meet again some day,' Bruce Watson said to her when they walked towards the terminal. 'It's a small world sometimes.'

Sarika did not answer him; she merely smiled aloofly and walked on without slackening her pace. There was a brief delay while she waited to collect her suitcases. Bruce appeared again at her side to lift them off the moving belt on to the trolley she had found. She wished silently that he would go away, but thanked him politely and walked on ahead. Going through Customs created no problem for her, and within a few minutes she was in the main arrival hall of the airport building.

The colourful and rowdy scene that met her eyes made her pulse quicken. She had always admired the Indian women for the dignity with which they wore their saris, and after so many months in England, it was a sight that warmed her heart. Her eyes searched the sea of dark-skinned faces. Someone would be there to meet her. She hoped it would be her father, but it would not surprise her if he had sent one of the junior members of his staff. She stood around, seconds lengthening into minutes, and sighed impatiently. How much longer would she still have to wait?

Perhaps she should take a taxi. The idea was beginning to appeal to her, but a little shiver raced up her spine before she could put her thoughts into action. She had the strangest feeling that someone was watching her, and the sensation was so strong that she found herself turning slowly as if some force beyond her control had taken charge of her body. A man in a blue open-necked shirt, white cotton slacks and canvas shoes was standing some distance from her. He was so tall that one would have difficulty ignoring him in a crowd, and the cotton of his shirt seemed to stretch too tightly across his powerful chest and wide shoulders. Her glance collided with his as he started walking towards her, and she found herself looking into eyes so dark they were almost black. They burned their way into her with a fierceness that held her immobile with something close to shock, and her pulse began to jerk in a totally unpredictable manner. Who was this man, and why was he walking towards her with those long, purposeful strides?

'Miss Maynesfield?' His voice was deep and gravelly, like the ominous roll of thunder, and his penetrating glance held hers compellingly despite her attempt to look away. His hair was as dark as his eyes, she noticed absently, and his deeply tanned features were rugged rather than handsome. She stared up at him in confusion, and his heavy eyebrows rose in a vaguely mocking manner. 'You are Sarika Maynesfield, aren't you?'

There was an almost animal maleness about this man that rocked her composure, and that aura of sexual vitality and strength that emanated from him made her intensely aware of her own femininity. No man had ever succeeded in doing that before, and the sensation was so disquieting that she had to make a near-physical attempt to pull herself together.

'Yes, I'm Sarika Maynesfield.' She hoped he had not heard the nervous tremor in her voice.

'Sean O'Connor,' he introduced himself abruptly, his assessing glance sending that little shiver racing up her spine once again. 'I was asked to collect you.'

Collect? Her status dropped at once from woman to bothersome package, and she could not decide whether she ought to be amused or annoyed.

'Do you work for my father?' she questioned him cautiously, her eyes on his strong, tanned forearms when he lifted her suitcases off the trolley, and she almost had to run to keep up with him when he strode towards the exit.

'In a manner of speaking.'

'What sort of answer is that?' she demanded confusedly.

'It's the only answer you're going to get at the moment.' He looked at her as if she was a spoiled, troublesome child instead of a woman of twenty-three. 'Now, if you don't mind, I'm in a hurry, and we're wasting valuable time.'

No one had ever spoken to her quite like that before and, fuming inwardly, she followed him out of the cool, air-conditioned building and into the hot, blazing sunshine. A second shock awaited her. Parked close to the entrance was the red Mercedes sports car her parents had given her for her twenty-first birthday, and Sean O'Connor was unlocking the boot and dumping her suitcases into it as if the car belonged to him. Her expression must have conveyed her annoyance when he glanced at her, and he raised his heavy eyebrows in sardonic amusement.

'I hope you don't mind,' he said smoothly, 'but I've commandeered your car while mine is being repaired.'

Sarika could not have answered him even if she had

wanted to. Her usually calm and serene temperament had suddenly deserted her, and she was speechless with an uncommon fury. She stood there rigidly while he slammed the boot shut and walked round to open the door on the passenger side. She wanted to tell him to go to the devil, that this was *her* car, and that *she* would drive, it, but one glance up into that rugged face made her realise that she would have to have all her wits about her if she wanted to involve herself in an argument with Sean O'Connor. There was something indefinable about him that warned her he was a man who was accustomed to getting what he wanted, and she was suddenly too tired to voice her resentment.

His hand touched her arm, making her aware of his impatience. It was a brief touch, but it was sufficient to send a charge of electricity through her that made her nerves tingle in response. Alarmed and disconcerted, she hastily got into the car to avoid a repetition, and moments later he was easing his long, muscular body into the driver's seat. The spacious interior shrank to a size that made her feel as if they had become closeted together in a cabin trunk, and the suggested intimacy of the situation made her sit stiffly in her seat when they drove away from the busy airport grounds towards the city.

Vendors were making their arduous way into the centre of Bombay at that early hour of the morning, and their carts were being pulled by lean-looking cattle with bells tied about their necks. Stalls were being erected in the quiet streets, but soon the city would become a hive of noisy activity.

Sarika had always enjoyed the drive from the airport to her home in Malabar Hills. She would feast her eyes on familiar sights and drink it all in like someone who had acquired a dreadful thirst, but Sean O'Connor's forceful and disturbing presence was much too distracting. She turned slightly in her seat, attempting to look calm and relaxed, and her glance was drawn irrevocably towards the man beside her. The straight nose and square, jutting jaw added a touch of ruthlessness to his rugged profile, but she was somehow not surprised by the hint of sensuality she glimpsed in the shape of his stern mouth. His big, well-shaped hands rested lightly on the wheel, but she knew without doubt that he was in perfect control of the vehicle. Her gaze dropped lower to his lean hips and muscled thighs encased in the tight-fitting cotton slacks, and there was a stirring inside her that was primitive and frightening. Her glance swept upwards again to his face, and for one electrifying second she found herself looking straight into his dark, mocking eyes.

Embarrassed at the knowledge that he had caught her staring, she twisted her head away before he could see the warm colour flooding her cheeks. She battled to regain her composure, and only when she had succeeded did she break the strained, awkward silence between them. 'My parents never told me that a new member had joined the Apex staff.'

'The past few months have been rather hectic for your father. Perhaps that's why he never got around to telling you.'

She recognised for the first time that slight American drawl in the way he spoke, and her curiosity deepened. 'How long have you been working for my father?'

'Long enough.'

'Do you always answer questions in that evasive manner?' she asked, suddenly angry, and his mocking gaze once again stabbed at her briefly.

'How long I've been with Apex is really none of your business. I'm here to drive you home, and not for the purpose of answering personal questions about myself.'

Sarika felt chastised, like a child who had been rapped over the knuckles for an offence, and she squirmed inwardly. 'I was merely attempting to make polite conversation.'

'Well, don't,' he said abruptly and rather rudely, Sarika thought, but it had the desired effect, and she lapsed into a silence that lasted the length of the hour and a half drive to her home.

Tense, and fuming inwardly, she sighed inaudibly with relief when the car shot up the long drive towards the pillared mansion which had been no more than a base, at times, which she returned to for her holidays. At first it had been boarding school, and later she had gone to university in England. The holidays had always seemed too brief for her to actually settle down, but Ayah had always been there, and it was Ayah who had succeeded most in making this palatial mansion feel like a home to Sarika.

She straightened her skirt when she got out of the car, and excitement made her hands flutter towards her hair to smooth the heavy weight of it away from her face and neck. Sean O'Connor witnessed this action when he lifted her suitcases and hand luggage out of the boot, and a cynical smile curved his mouth.

'You look ravishing enough despite your long, tiring flight,' he mocked her when she glanced at him questioningly, 'but I'm sure you know that without being told.'

Sarika glared at him with a rising sense of mutiny. 'Do you dislike women in general, Mr O'Connor, or is there something about me *personally* that you happen to dislike?'

'I dislike spoiled little girls who think they can get away with murder by simply fluttering their long eyelashes in the right direction.'

He spoke with such a savagery that she actually backed a pace away from him. A spoiled little girl, was she? Bitterness surged like gall into her mouth, and she was still trying to formulate a reply when Ayah's ample figure emerged from the house. She was wearing her customary white sari to signify that she was a woman in mourning, and it wafted about her legs as she hurried down the steps towards Sarika.

Her anger and irritation forgotten for the moment, Sarika almost fell into Ayah's outstretched arms, and that faint and familiar smell of incense which clung to this woman was an added welcome home. They hugged each other profusely, laughing and crying at the same time.

'Oh, Ayah,' Sarika smiled through her tears when they finally held each other at arm's length. 'I really missed you, and it's so good to be home at last!'

'Pyaari!' Darling. The endearment spilled naturally from Ayah's lips, and there was a loving warmth in her beautiful dark eyes when she studied Sarika critically. 'You must be exhausted after your long flight, and you have lost weight.'

'I haven't really,' Sarika protested uncomfortably while she was aware of Sean O'Connor's black eyes observing them with a mixture of amused and cynical interest.

'I'll fatten you up in a week,' promised Ayah, then she turned and smiled at the man standing a few paces away from them. 'I know you are in a hurry to get back to the office, Sean, so if you will leave Sarika's suitcases in the hall I will instruct one of the servants to take further care of them.'

Sean? Ayah's familiar use of this man's name made Sarika glance at the older woman enquiringly, but Ayah seemed not to notice as she ushered Sarika into the house. Sean O'Connor followed close behind, and Sarika felt again that strange little shiver racing up her spine as if his eyes were burning holes into her back. Her suitcases were dumped unceremoniously on the black and white marble-tiled floor of the hall and, raising his hand in a brief salute to Ayah, he strode out of the house and down the steps to get into the Mercedes as if he owned it.

The man was infuriating, and incredibly disturbing. He was also something of a mystery. She would question Ayah about him later, but first she wanted to see her parents. 'Where are Mum and Dad, Ayah? They did remember that I'd be arriving today, didn't they?'

'They are not here, *pyaari.*'

'What do you mean, they're not here?'

'Later, Sarika,' the older woman brushed aside her anxious query. 'Go upstairs, take a shower, and change into something comfortable. I will bring up a pot of tea, and then we will talk.'

Sarika knew that tone of voice, and she knew also the futility of pressing this woman for an answer when she was not ready to give it. Sighing inwardly, she did as she was told and went upstairs to her room.

A pleasant surprise awaited her there. The room was not as she had left it eight months ago. The furnishings were a cool blue instead of rose-pink, the slatted doors of the wooden wall-cupboard had been painted white, and a matching dressing table replaced the old-fashioned teak dresser. The two comfortable chairs in front of the large window had also been covered in a soft blue material to give the room a new sophisticated and modern appearance, and everything which could possibly have reminded her of her unfortunate experience with Gary had been removed.

Everything else was temporarily swept from her mind as she stood there taking in the delightful appearance of her old room with tears in her eyes. This was Ayah's contribution in helping her to forget the unpleasant past, and Sarika loved her all the more for it.

Aware suddenly that she was hot and sticky, Sarika went into the adjacent bathroom and stripped down to her skin. She stepped into the shower cubicle, and the cool jet of water against her body was soothing and refreshing. She stood like that for some time before she soaped herself and washed her hair, and she felt considerably better when she had dried herself and put on clean undies. With a small towel wrapped about her head, she slipped her arms into a green silk robe and returned to her bedroom to find her suitcases standing at the foot of the bed with the polished brass bars at the head.

Sarika had dried her hair and was brushing it vigorously when Ayah walked into the room with a tray of tea. Their eyes met in the mirror and they smiled at each other fondly. 'I like the new furnishings, Ayah. It was kind of you to go to all the trouble.'

'I didn't do it all on my own,' Ayah protested modestly, placing the tray on the low table between the two chairs at the window. 'Cara *bhenji* chose the curtains and the fine silk bedspread, and Dave *bhaiji* ordered the dressing table to be made to match the wall-cupboard.'

Sister Cara and *brother* Dave—that had always been Ayah's respectful way of addressing Sarika's parents. Sarika studied the older woman closely and decided that, in all the years she had known her, she had not changed very much. She had never seen Ayah's nicely rounded body dressed in anything other than her white cotton saris, and she had always generated a warm and tender motherly affection which had made Sarika feel wanted and cherished. Her hair was a little greyer, but oiled as usual, and combed back into a neat bun in the nape of her neck.

'Tell me about Mum and Dad, Ayah?' Sarika repeated her query with a little more urgency on this occasion. 'Where are they, and why aren't they here this morning to welcome me home?'

'Beti . . .' Ayah always called Sarika *daughter* when she was deeply concerned, or when she had unpleasant news to pass on to her, and Sarika steeled herself against whatever blow was to follow. 'I'm sorry, but your parents left yesterday morning to join the Parkers on their yacht for a three-week cruise along the coast towards Karachi. It was something they could not cancel, and they asked me to tell you that they would look forward to seeing you on their return.'

For Sarika it was the final disappointment in a long list of disappointments, and this time she could not simply sit back and accept it as calmly as she had always done in the past. 'They could have waited, Ayah!' she cried out, leaping to her feet in a burst of anger. 'They could have waited *one* more day, but this yacht trip was obviously more important to them than my return home. Oh, how I hate them for always thinking only of themselves!'

'Now, now, Sarika!' Ayah rebuked her gently as she came to Sarika and gripped her arms. 'You know you don't really hate your parents, and the three weeks will pass so quickly that you will wonder why you made such a fuss about them not being here.'

Sarika drew a deep, calming breath. She did not cry this time; she had shed enough tears in the past in which to drown herself. Her childhood years had been lonely years, and she had cried herself to sleep most nights. Ayah had showered her with love and attention, but it never quite eased that terrible pain deep down inside her, nor did it fill that void left by her parents' lack of concern.

'You're right as usual, Ayah,' she sighed, letting the tension flow from her as she allowed herself to be led to a chair. 'They'll be home before I know it.'

Ayah poured their tea, and they drank it in silence until Ayah left her alone to rest. Sarika drew the curtains to darken her room, and realised that, in her disappointment at not finding her parents at home, she had forgotten to question Ayah about Sean O'Connor. His mocking eyes and cynical smile taunted her, and she felt certain that she would not sleep—but, surprisingly, she did.

CHAPTER TWO

THE sun was setting over the city which lay in the distance, and Sarika stood looking out of her bedroom window until the lengthening shadows had deepened into darkness in the spacious, well-kept garden below. It was time to go down to dinner, but the thought of dining alone did not appeal to her. Ayah would, of course, dine with her, but Sarika had imagined her first evening at home quite differently, only to discover that it would be no different from any of the others. She had hoped that her parents would be proud of her achievement, that their inability to attend her graduation would have made them feel duty bound, at least, to spend this one evening with her, but Sarika should have known that nothing like that would ever happen. They had always been too busy chasing after life's pleasures to care about her. Ayah, after all, was here to look after her, and with that they exonerated themselves of all responsibility.

The garden below was now in total darkness, and Sarika drew the curtains across the window, standing for a moment with her head bowed and her hands clutching at the material before she turned away with a sigh to switch on the bedside light. She felt lonely and depressed, but the feeling was not new to her, and she knew she dared not dwell on it. Self-pity was a crippling emotion that distorted one's outlook on life, and she would not become a slave to it.

Her mind conjured up Sean O'Connor's image. Sarika did not want to think about him, but he was not a man one could meet one moment and forget the next. He had, most annoyingly, intruded on her waking thoughts most of that day, and this time she could not banish him from her mind. He had called her a spoiled little girl, and it was as if he had taken a delight in striking her where it hurt most. A little girl she was not, and spoiled she never had been. She had been given everything that money could buy, but she had never asked for it, and neither had she revelled in it. Since her eighteenth birthday there had been men who had considered her appearance and her father's wealth as two of her best assets, but Sean O'Connor seemed to actually despise her for it. When Sarika allowed herself time to pause for consideration, she found that she had to admit his manner was refreshing, and somewhat intriguing. She must remember to find out more about him from Ayah, she decided as she left her room and went downstairs.

Sarika crossed the hall towards the living-room, the heels of her white sandals clicking on the marble floor. She felt rested and relaxed, but when she entered the living-room, she stood rooted to the spot with her heart leaping into her throat, and her body tense with indignation. Sean O'Connor stood in front of the cabinet with its inlaid wood of Eastern origin, and he was helping himself to her father's best whisky. He turned, the ice tinkling in his glass, and for several seconds she was incapable of speech while his dark eyes travelled slowly down the length of her and burned their insolent way through the fine silk of her amber-coloured dress. His glance lingered on the gentle curve of her breasts and hips, making her feel oddly naked, and an angry flush stained her cheeks.

'What do you think you're doing?' she demanded tritely even though her subconscious registered the fact that he looked magnificent in an immaculate beige suit with a wine-red shirt left unbuttoned to expose his sun-browned throat and part of his hair-roughened chest. His black hair was brushed back severely instead of curling on to his broad forehead as it had done that morning, and black eyes observed her intently from beneath arched brows.

'I should have thought it was obvious,' he smiled derisively, indicating the glass in his hand.

'You apparently had my father's permission to use my car,' she launched into an icy attack. 'But is he aware of the fact that you not only invade his home while he's away, but also his drinks cabinet?'

'Your father is very much aware of my presence in this house.' His eyes glittered with mockery. 'I've been living here for the past six months.'

'You live here?' she almost choked on the words. 'In this house?'

'I have the suite in the east wing.'

The suite in the east wing had always been reserved for important and highly honoured guests. Would her father install one of his employees in that particular suite?

'I don't believe it!' she snapped suspiciously.

'Suit yourself.' Sean O'Connor shrugged his wide shoulders. 'May I pour you a sherry?'

He did not wait for her to reply, and she found herself staring a little stupefied at his broad back, and the way his hair curled slightly on to his collar. 'Why was I not told? Why did no one mention it?'

'It must have slipped their minds.' He turned and lessened the distance between them with a few long, easy strides. 'Your sherry.'

She accepted the glass from him in silence and swallowed down a small mouthful of sherry to steady her nerves, but Sean O'Connor was standing too close to her for comfort. So close, in fact, that the tantalising scent of his masculine cologne stirred her senses in the most alarming way, and she turned away from him to subside into one of the comfortably padded chairs.

'I presume you're staying here until you find something more suitable,' she resumed their conversation while she arranged the skirt of her dress about her knees.

'I think this place suits my needs admirably,' he replied, lowering himself into the chair facing hers and stretching his long, muscular legs out in front of him so that the tips of his polished leather shoes almost touched hers.

'In other words,' she responded scathingly, 'you intend to stay on and make ill-use of my father's hospitality.'

'Why not?' he mocked her. 'This house is big enough to accommodate a dozen people without anyone having to fall over someone else's feet.'

'That's beside the point.'

'The point is, Sarika Maynesfield, that you're a self-opinionated little bitch, and you can't bear the thought of your parents' attention being diverted from you for one moment.' The attack was so unexpected that she simply sat there staring at him while he continued to lash her cruelly. 'You've always been spoiled by your parents, and they've stupidly danced attendance to you, but with me around their attention is going to be divided, and that's what's eating you up inside.'

Sarika could not decide whether she ought to laugh or cry. She had a strong desire to do both, but instead she sat there staring at him through a mist of pain which she veiled with her long, silky lashes. She wanted to defend herself; she wanted to tell him how completely wrong he was about her, but defending herself could lead to the baring of her soul, and anger came to her rescue before she made a complete fool of herself. Sean O'Connor was free to think what he wished. What did she care, after all?

The atmosphere was strained and heavy with antagonism. She sensed that he was waiting for her to strike back, but she chose to ignore his obvious challenge, and it was at that moment that Ayah floated into the room in a fresh white sari to relieve some of the tension.

'Dinner is served,' Ayah announced, and her glance went from Sean O'Connor to rest sternly on Sarika. 'I shall expect to see an empty plate this evening after the way you nibbled at the lunch I had sent up to your room.'

Sarika rose to her feet and was surprised to find that her legs were shaky, but she managed somehow to smile. 'I shall do my best, Ayah.'

Sean O'Connor had also risen to his feet, and he drained his glass quickly before gesturing towards Sarika's sherry. 'May I top up your glass, Miss Maynesfield?'

'No, thank you, Mr O'Connor.'

'Now what is all this formality?' Ayah exploded with mock severity. 'In this house there has never been such a thing, and you are well aware of that, Sarika.'

Sarika chose not to answer her, and it was Sean who broke the awkward silence. 'Would you like a small sherry, Ayah?'

'Sherry goes to my head,' Ayah scowled at him playfully, 'and well you know it.'

'In that case,' he put down his glass and crooked his arms, 'may I escort you ladies to the dining-room?'

Ayah linked her arm through his without hesitation, and Sarika, standing on his right, had no option but to do the same. She could feel the hard, bunched-up muscles through the thinness of his jacket, and touching him like that sent an electrifying sensation charging through her. Her nerves vibrated, her pulse quickened, and she removed her hand from his arm the instant they entered the dining-room. She caught a glimpse of his mocking glance as he escorted Ayah to her chair and helped her into it, and Sarika did not wait for his assistance. She sat down in her usual place, expecting him to sit down next to Ayah, but instead he seated himself at the head of the table where her father always sat.

Sarika seethed inwardly. The effrontery of the man! He was behaving as if the house belonged to him, and as if she was a mere guest in it! She glanced at Ayah, expecting to see a similar reaction, but Ayah behaved as if it was the most natural thing for Sean O'Connor to assume the position of the head of the house. Sarika felt totally bewildered. What exactly was going on in this house?

Ayah served the consommé. It was not a favourite of Sarika's, but Sean O'Connor appeared to enjoy it, and he downed two bowls of it to Sarika and Ayah's one. Ayah rang the bell for one of the kitchen staff. The soup bowls were removed, and Ayah lifted the lids off the serving dishes while Sarika took a sip of her sherry. Sean was served first, while Sarika stared at the excellent cuisine as if she had not seen food in months. There was spiced rice with peri-peri chicken covered with a tangy sauce, a beef and onion stew which had been marinated in wine, and meatballs flavoured with nutmeg, olives and various cheeses. There was also a bowl of yoghurt into which had been added cucumber cubes, dill and garlic.

'Your plate, Sarika,' Ayah captured her attention, and Sarika watched in dismay as Ayah loaded her plate with a substantial helping of everything.

'Ayah, I can't possibly eat all that!' protested Sarika, but Ayah was suddenly conveniently deaf.

Sarika stared in dismay at the heaped plate of food in front of her. She would never manage to finish it all. Something made her raise her glance, and she found herself looking directly into Sean O'Connor's mocking, challenging eyes. *Damn* the man! Did he have to make everything seem like a challenge to her? She picked up her knife and fork and started eating, and it was after the first few mouthfuls that she realised how hungry she actually was. The last decent meal she had had was on the eve of her departure from Paris, and that was a week ago. Ignoring Sean O'Connor's amused glances, Sarika continued eating, and when Ayah rang for the kitchen staff to clear the table, Sarika lowered her knife and fork to her empty plate with an involuntary smile of satisfaction lifting the corners of her mouth.

'That was an excellent meal, Ayah,' Sarika complimented the woman seated opposite her.

'And I echo that,' added Sean O'Connor. 'I shall

have to watch myself in future, or you'll have *me* picking up weight instead of Sarika.'

The sound of her name sounded strange and oddly exciting on his lips, but it was the smile he bestowed on Ayah that held Sarika temporarily spellbound. It softened the harsh contours of his rugged features in a way that made Sarika wish he would smile at her like that just once. It was a crazy desire, and she was angry with herself the next instant for daring to think about something so ridiculous.

'It's such a warm night,' Ayah interrupted her thoughts. 'If you would both go out on to the terrace then I shall have your coffee served there.'

Sarika started to say that she would rather go up to her room, but Sean O'Connor was already standing beside her chair to assist her to her feet. 'Come, Sarika,' he said. 'Coffee on the terrace will be an excellent way to finish off such a delightful meal.'

For a fraction of a second there was a strange look in Ayah's eyes when Sarika glanced at her, but it was replaced so swiftly by an encouraging smile that Sarika could almost believe she had imagined it as she left the table in silence and walked out on to the terrace which overlooked the pool and tennis court.

The air was warm and scented, and Sarika breathed it deeply into her lungs as she stood with her hands resting on the low wall. Sean O'Connor lowered himself into a cane chair, and it creaked protestingly beneath his weight. He looked relaxed when she turned slightly to observe him unobtrusively, but she sensed an alertness in him which could make him leap into action at a moment's notice. Her body stiffened with an unfamiliar tension, and her nerves began to quiver. She was convinced that she looked outwardly calm, but she could not shake off the humiliating suspicion that this man was very much aware of how she was reacting to his presence.

'We were having an interesting conversation before dinner.' The sound of his deep, gravelly voice made her nerves coil themselves into knots. 'I think it would be even more interesting to continue with it.'

Both the living-room and dining-room doors stood wide open, and they shed sufficient light out on to the terrace for Sarika to see his rugged features quite clearly. She also had to remember that she was facing directly into the light, and she masked that feeling of distaste that rose in her as she said sharply, 'I don't wish to pursue the subject.'

'Why not?' he mocked her, stretching his long legs comfortably out in front of him and leaning back in his chair. 'Was I getting too close to the core of your problem for comfort?'

She winced inwardly, and clenched her hands at her sides. What was it about this man that he could arouse her to such a terrifying peak of anger? 'Mr O'Connor, I——'

'Sean,' he interrupted her smoothly. 'My name is Sean, remember?'

'Sean . . .' she repeated hesitantly, feeling like a balloon which had been partially deflated. 'You jumped to a few nasty conclusions about me, and I don't think you had the right to do that without knowing me better.'

'So I jumped to a few nasty conclusions, did I?' His mouth twisted derisively, and his dark eyes glittered harshly in the subdued light. 'You explain to me, then, why you don't like the idea of having me in this house?'

Sarika was saved from answering immediately when a young Punjabi girl stepped out on to the terrace with a tray of coffee, and Sarika stared absently at the girl in the straight blue tunic of mid-calf length with matching pants fitting tightly about the slender ankles. The girl walked silently on soft-soled sandals, and when she turned to leave Sarika glimpsed the long dark plait hanging down her back.

Relieved to have something to do, Sarika poured their coffee, and left Sean to help himself to cream and sugar. She sat down in the chair beside the low table and drank her coffee, but her mind was whirling with thoughts. How did she feel about Sean O'Connor's presence in her home? She was puzzled, and perhaps also a little indignant, she had to admit to herself. She was also intensely curious.

'I'm still waiting for an explanation,' Sean reminded her, lighting a cheroot when they had finished their coffee, and blowing the aromatic smoke through his nostrils.

'It's not that I like or dislike the idea of you living here,' she answered carefully. 'I simply find it . . . strange.'

'That's not a very good explanation, but I'll accept it for the moment,' he mocked her, and she turned her head away when she felt herself blushing like a child caught out on a lie.

He smoked his cheroot in silence, but she felt restless beneath the steady probing of his eyes. If she jumped up now and went to her room he would find yet another reason to mock her, so she got up with as much casualness as she could muster, and walked slowly towards a section of the terrace which was in partial darkness. She felt safer there, as if the shadows offered her some protection, but she remained tense and wary.

There was not a breeze to mar the stillness of that oddly perfect night. The city lights flickered in the distance, and Sarika forgot briefly that she was not alone as she wished that she could see beyond those lights. She wondered about her parents as they cruised up along the coast in a yacht, and wished she could know what they were doing. It was a beautiful, balmy night for sitting out on the deck, and the visibility at sea would be good.

Sarika raised her glance towards the velvety, star-studded sky and, without realising it, she voiced the remaining fragment of her thoughts. 'The moon is full, and it's such a marvellous night.'

'And a very provocative sight you present standing there in the moonlight,' drawled Sean, his American accent more pronounced, and she spun round a little startled to see him strolling towards her with his fingers dipped into the pockets of his pants. He had removed his jacket, and his wine-red shirt accentuated his powerful shoulders. 'Are you as innocent as you pretend to be, or are you trying to tempt me, Sarika?'

'I wouldn't want to tempt you if you were the last man on earth!' she bit out the words, her heart pounding wildly in her breast. 'You're not my type.'

That was the wrong thing to say—she knew it! And Sean did not let the opportunity pass to goad her.

'What kind of man is your type, then?' he laughed softly, but it was not a pleasant laugh, and she leaned back against the pillar when he stopped no more than a pace away from her. 'Do you go for the type you can pick up when you're interested, and drop the minute you're bored?' he probed derisively.

'Most certainly not!' she gasped indignantly. 'I have no interest in men, or in any kind of relationship which involves a man.'

'Don't put on that ice-maiden act with me, Sarika,' he laughed again, and the sound jarred her nerves. 'I know women, and I suspect that underneath that layer of ice there lurks an unawakened but passionate woman who's simply crying out for the right man to come along.'

'And he'll sweep me off my feet, and I'll melt into his arms?' she retorted contemptuously. 'Oh, don't make me laugh!'

'Perhaps you would like to indulge in a little experiment?'

'With you?' she asked sarcastically, her heart beginning to thud uncomfortably against her ribs.

'Why not?'

'No, thanks!' she snapped.

'You make that sound like a challenge, Sarika, and I've always been a sucker for challenges.'

He leaned towards her, one hand resting on the low wall beside her, and she shrank against the pillar in an attempt to escape that overpowering aura of maleness which seemed to reach out with the threat to envelop her. 'If you touch me I'll scream!'

'What are you afraid of, Sarika?' he mocked her.

'I'm not afraid of you, if that's what you're thinking.'

'Then you must be afraid of yourself,' he hit on the awful truth. 'Are you afraid you might enjoy my touch?'

'I know I shall loathe it!' she hissed fiercely, warning bells clanging in her mind. She knew she had to get away from him, but she stood trapped against the pillar and the low wall, and Sean's large body looked as immovable as a rock.

'Let's find out, shall we?' he laughed throatily as he towered over her, and her mouth went dry as fear clamoured through her.

'No, I don't want——'

Her protest died in her throat when his big hand captured hers, and the shock of his touch sent a paralysing current of electricity through her that left her powerless to resist when he raised her hand to his lips. His mouth explored the delicate network of veins along the inner side of her wrist, and the erotic caress of his tongue against her palm sent a charge of fiery sensations surging through her body. It frightened her that he could awaken such unfamiliar feelings, but his compelling eyes held hers captive, and she stood motionless, scarcely daring to breathe.

'You were saying, Sarika?' he mocked her, his lips trailing up along the inside of her arm and creating havoc with her emotions.

Her pulse was racing madly, and she had the awful feeling that she was sinking into a pool of sensual awareness from which there was no escape. He had no right to make her feel this way, and from the recesses of her mind came the warning that she had to stop him before it was too late. 'I—I think this experiment has—has gone far enough.'

'This is only the beginning.'

'You're wasting your time,' she argued stiffly, trying feebly to pull away from him, but he seemed to anticipate her actions, and a heavy arm was clamped about her waist like a vice.

'Time is never wasted when it's spent like this,' murmured Sean, his deep, gravelly voice acting like a soothing caress to her quivering nerves as he drew her inexorably closer until her body came into contact with his tall, hard frame.

It was a shattering experience to feel the contours of his male body against her own. To make matters worse it felt as if she belonged there, and a strange weakness invaded her limbs when he took her hand and pushed it inside his shirt until the hair-roughened warmth of his chest was against her palm. He was encouraging an intimacy between them which should have made her want to pull her hand away, but instead her fingers seemed to take a delight in exploring the texture of his skin.

This was madness! She hardly knew this man, and he was making her do things which were quite contrary to her usual behaviour. 'Ayah may come out and——'

'You know Ayah's routine even better than I do,' he interrupted her weak protestation as he lifted the heavy strands of hair away from her heated face and curled his fingers into its silky weight at the base of her skull to tilt her head back. 'Ayah will remain in the kitchen until the servants have left it spotless, and then she'll retire to her room for an hour to say her prayers, or whatever it is she does there.'

He lowered his head, his lips seeking her exposed throat, and the touch of his tongue was like fire against her responsive skin as he blazed a trail of searing, exploratory kisses down to that sensitive hollow at the base of her throat where her pulse was throbbing wildly. His hand was warm through the silk of her dress as he slid it up along the hollow of her spine and down again to draw her hips closer into the curve of his hard body. He was arousing electrifying sensations that seemed to heat her blood and make it flow at a swifter pace through her veins, and her resistance began to crumble dangerously.

'Please stop it!' she begged in a husky, unfamiliar voice, her fingers curling into a fist against his broad chest in a futile attempt to push him away.

'You're trembling,' he said, his lips brushing against her ear, 'and you can't attribute that to the weather.'

'I think I hate you!' she cried out in protest against his mockery and his obvious expertise as a lover.

'Hate is a positive emotion I have no objection to.'

'Sean . . .' She was sounding horribly weak, and she hated him all the more when she realised that she was in danger of betraying herself. 'Let me go!'

'I haven't completed the experiment yet,' he admonished her lightly.

As far as Sarika was concerned, the experiment had gone beyond all sense of decency. She had met Sean O'Connor for the first time that morning, but somehow he had succeeded in weaving a spell about her which filled her with the strange desire to surrender herself to the fiery emotions he was arousing so expertly. His lips were trailing along the edge of her jaw to linger for a tantalising moment at the corner of her mouth. He teased and aroused her, and his hands slid coaxingly over her body until the last fragment of her resistance crumbled.

She wanted him to kiss her. She wanted it so badly at that moment that her hands slid up over his chest to become locked in his hair which she found surprisingly soft to the touch, and a choked cry of surrender escaped her as she drew his head down to hers.

His sensuous mouth closed over her parted lips, and Sarika lost her final grip on sanity. She had never before encountered such a searing passion which excited her and lifted her almost beyond herself. It unleashed a wildness in her which was totally alien to her nature, and her body was yielding and pliant in his arms as he drew her closer still to his hard, muscular frame until she was aware of his own burning desire for her. His hands roamed in a slow, sensual caress down her back and up again to cup her breasts through the silky bodice of her dress, and the aching sweetness of his touch sent a wave of pleasure storming through her that made her wish it would never end. She was allowing this man intimacies which she had never allowed anyone before, but her mind was no longer in control of her body, and she was aware only of clinging weakly to his broad shoulders to steady herself in this dizzy, ecstatic world she had been plunged into.

Sarika was trembling like a fragile reed in the breeze when Sean finally released her. Her heart was racing and her breath came fast over her parted lips as she stood swaying in front of him. She felt strangely disembodied as she groped for the pillar behind her and leaned against it for support while she stared up into Sean's shadowed face. What was he thinking? Was he also experiencing this feeling of incredulous awe at the fierce emotions which had erupted between them?

'Well, that was quite something, wasn't it?' he drawled. 'The ice-maiden has fire in her veins after all!'

The mockery in his voice stabbed into the very essence of her being like a heated blade, and she came to her senses with a sickening jolt that made her react in a manner which was totally out of character. Her hand flew up and caught him a stinging blow across the cheek that made his head jerk slightly. The silence that followed was almost deafening, but it was broken seconds later by the low rumble of his mocking laughter.

'Does that make you feel better after discovering that you have desires just like any other woman?' he taunted her.

'You're disgusting!' she hissed, and fled indoors with his mocking laughter following her as she ran across the hall and up the stairs to her room.

She slammed the door shut behind her, but his laughter still echoed tormentingly in her mind, and a low cry of fury escaped Sarika's quivering, swollen lips as she flung herself across her bed. He had been playing with her; he had been testing her, and the result had proved him right. She was a woman who had been crying out for the right man to come along and awaken those slumbering emotions inside her, but . . . oh, God, she had not wanted it to be someone like Sean O'Connor! She wished she would never have to face him again, but she knew that was impossible. They were living in the same house, eating at the same table, and God only knew what her father had had in mind when he had taken this man into their home.

Sean had torn down her carefully erected barriers with the ease of a man who had obviously had plenty of experience with women, and her lack of resistance nauseated her when she recalled every humiliating detail of the incidents which had occurred out on the terrace. She felt embarrassed and deeply ashamed of the way she had behaved, and she cringed inwardly when she remembered how she had encouraged him to kiss her.

Sarika groaned and buried her hot face deeper into the pillow. Was she ever going to live this down? Would he ever let her forget? The memory of his mocking laughter still tormented her, and she knew she would have to stay out of his way as much as possible in future.

There was an element of danger in associating with a man like Sean O'Connor, and she had sensed this the moment their eyes had met at the airport. He had aroused a physical reaction which she had never encountered with any other man, and it should have acted as a warning to stay away from him. What, she wondered, had prompted his actions this evening? He had made it clear that he disliked her, but he had also shown her that she was capable of making him want her. Why? And why had she responded to him in a way she had not done before with any man . . . not even Gary? Sean had awakened wild, alien emotions which frightened her, and she was infinitely wary of something so powerful that it could make her lose control in the shameful way she had done that evening.

Sarika had succeeded to some extent in regaining her composure when Ayah came to her room for a few minutes later that evening. Sarika had wanted to question Ayah about Sean, but she was not thinking rationally. Her mind was still in a nervous turmoil, and it kept her awake for some hours on that disastrous first night at home.

CHAPTER THREE

SARIKA awoke the following morning with the premonition that something unpleasant was going to happen. She had never experienced anything like this before, and it left her feeling disturbed and uneasy long after she had washed and changed into a white cheesecloth top that hugged her body, and blue denim shorts that accentuated the attractive length of her smooth, shapely legs.

She walked barefoot to the window, and was just in time to catch a glimpse of Sean striding out of the house towards a Land Rover parked in the long, decorative driveway. He was dressed casually in blue, his powerful shoulders swinging slightly as he moved, and when he climbed into the Land Rover she could not help but think that the vehicle suited the man. They were both rugged and strong and . . . dependable?

He glanced up unexpectedly as if he suspected he was being observed, and Sarika leapt angrily away from the window with a pounding heart. It would be the last straw if he had seen her! '*Damn* the man!' she muttered to herself, her hand against her breast where her heart would not cease its wild tempo. 'Did he have to be here to spoil what little joy there was left in my homecoming?'

Sarika calmed herself sufficiently to comb her hair back into a ponytail, and she pushed her feet into low-heeled sandals before she went downstairs. Ayah was in the kitchen discussing the luncheon and dinner menu with the Indian chef, but, despite the lightness of Sarika's step, Ayah turned at once to face her.

'Good morning, *pyaari*,' she smiled welcomingly. 'I hope you have slept well?'

'Very well, thank you,' Sarika assured her, and that

was not entirely a lie. It had taken her several hours to settle down, but she had eventually drifted into a dreamless sleep.

'What will you have for breakfast?'

'A cup of tea will do, Ayah.'

'A cup of tea!' Ayah exclaimed, flinging her hands into the air in a gesture of despair as she turned to the chef for support. 'Look at her, Prakash. She has become as thin as a rake since her last visit, and all she wants for breakfast is a cup of tea!'

Prakash nodded in serious agreement, but there was a smile in the eyes that met Sarika's as Ayah pulled out a chair at the kitchen table.

'Sit down!' she ordered sharply, pointing an authoritative finger at the chair, and Sarika found that old habits die hard.

She obeyed the command and sat down meekly while Ayah snapped out orders to the chef. With a swiftness that never failed to amaze Sarika, she was served with fried eggs, bacon, toast and marmalade, and one glance at Ayah's stony features made her eat her breakfast without uttering a word of protest.

Ayah's smile of satisfaction followed Sarika when she finally left the kitchen, and Sarika had to admit to herself that the substantial breakfast had dispensed with that hollow feeling at the pit of her stomach.

She wandered listlessly through the house, touching this, touching that as if to renew old acquaintances, but she lingered for some considerable time in the master bedroom. She had done that often as a child. It had, in some strange way, made her feel close to her parents when she stood surrounded by their personal possessions, and she felt that way now. On the dressing-table stood a white porcelain bowl decorated with tiny blue flowers in which her mother always kept some of her inexpensive trinkets, and on a low table between two high-backed chairs was a box of her father's favourite cigars. Sarika felt her throat tighten with a mixture of resentment and longing, and she left the room hastily without having disturbed anything.

Down the passage to her left was the white panelled door of the suite in the east wing. A stab of curiosity made her walk towards it, but she changed her mind abruptly when her fingers touched the brass handle, and she quickened her pace as she retraced her steps. Invading that suite might have given her an insight into Sean O'Connor's true character. But did she really want to know that much about him? she asked herself as she went downstairs.

Sarika had not yet found an answer to that query when she encountered Ayah in the cupboard-sized room which had been turned into an office. 'I'm going for a long walk, but I'll be back for lunch.'

'Don't go too far, and take care,' Ayah warned as she had always done, and a warmth stole about Sarika's heart.

'Don't worry,' she smiled, leaning over to kiss the rounded cheek of the older woman before she walked out of the house and into the sunshine.

She had been away for so long that everything looked different somehow, or perhaps she was looking at everything with renewed interest after her lengthy stay in England. In Bombay everyone drove on the right side of the road, but that appeared to be the only fragment of organisation among the general chaos. The roads were thronged with cars of all makes, and each one was crammed with people going about their business, or sightseeing. Bullock carts, loaded with fruit and vegetables, moved slowly in among the speeding traffic. Horns blared at the obstruction they caused, but neither the vendor with his cart nor the pedestrians took much notice. The vendor would take his time moving his cart out of the way, and the drivers would curse and wave their fists in frustration. This was Bombay, Sarika smiled to herself as she strolled through the gates of the Hanging Gardens which were no more than a block away from her home.

She walked around for some time, drinking in the beauty of her surroundings before she sought out the circular marble pavilion in the centre of the garden. The scent of jasmine was cloying the air as she entered the pavilion, and she inhaled the sweet fragrance while she drank in the peaceful atmosphere. Pigeons fluttered around the fountain which had been built specially for them, and Sarika felt herself relax completely while she stood watching their antics. This was her favourite spot in the Hanging Gardens, and this was where she had always sought refuge in the past when she was troubled, or disturbed about something. The peace and tranquillity had never failed to calm her, and it did not fail on this occasion.

'Sarika!' She swung round at the sound of her name to find herself confronted by a young Indian woman who stood at the entrance of the pavilion smiling at her rather reproachfully. 'I have been trying for some time to attract your attention, but you were lost in thought,' she complained.

'Jaishree!' Sarika exclaimed with delight as she stepped forward to embrace her friend.

'It is so good to see you again, Sarika,' Jaishree smiled at her. 'When did you arrive?'

'Yesterday morning.'

'Too late to see your parents.'

It was a statement, not a query, and Sarika's expression sobered. 'Unfortunately, yes.'

'I have so much to tell you,' Jaishree changed the subject hastily. 'I am going to be married.'

'Oh, but that's wonderful!' smiled Sarika.

'I am going to be very busy this weekend, but you and I must get together next weekend for lunch, or something, and I will tell you everything then.'

'That would be nice,' Sarika agreed.

'I will call you next week to make a definite arrangement, but now I must rush,' Jaishree excused herself.

'I shall look forward to hearing from you,' Sarika

assured her, and moments later she was standing alone in the pavilion while her friend walked hurriedly towards the exit of the Hanging Gardens.

It had been good to see Jaishree again. She was the daughter of a friend of Ayah's, but, much to the older generation's annoyance, Jaishree was modern in her thinking and in her way of dress. Sarika had known Jaishree since they were children, and she would not be surprised to learn that Jaishree was marrying a man she loved rather than someone her parents had selected for her.

Sarika's mood had lightened considerably when she eventually left the gardens and walked back to the house. She glanced at her watch and realised that she had been gone from home for more than two hours. Ayah might be concerned about her, but Sarika did not let this thought disturb her. It felt as if she was taking with her some of the peace and tranquillity she had encountered in the gardens, and she did not quicken her pace.

If Ayah was concerned about her, then she did not show it, but she did frown disapprovingly when Sarika told her of her meeting with Jaishree.

'Jaishree is still as stubborn as always,' announced Ayah crossly. 'The husband her parents chose for her is not good enough for that young lady, and she has insisted on marrying a man whose parents her family have no knowledge of.'

'It's old-fashioned not to let a girl choose her own husband,' Sarika laughed at the discovery that her suspicions had been correct. 'I've always known that Jaishree would never marry a man unless she loved him, and was sure that he loved her.'

'Love!' snorted Ayah. 'It is important that a girl marries a man she can respect, and a man who will take good care of her. Love will come later.'

A slight frown appeared on Sarika's smooth brow. 'Is there something wrong with the man Jaishree has chosen?'

'He comes from a wealthy home, but no one seems to know anything about his family,' Ayah complained, 'and they will be meeting this weekend for the first time.'

So *that* was why Jaishree had said that she would be busy this weekend. Her parents were going to meet the parents of her future husband, and Sarika had no doubt it was going to be a rather tense meeting until they had succeeded in summing each other up successfully.

After a light lunch Sarika went up to her room to rest for a while, and she actually slept for an hour. She was restless and hot when she got up, and she changed quickly into her green bikini before going down to the pool for a swim.

The water looked cool and inviting and, leaving her towelling robe draped over a chair, she dived into the crystal clear water and swam with long, easy strokes to the opposite side. The coolness of the water against her body was refreshing, and she lingered in the pool for some time before she swam to the side and got out. She wrung the water out of her hair with a twisting motion and flicked it back over her shoulder before she sat down on the recliner and allowed the sun to dry her body. Her skin had paled during those long months in England, but she tanned easily, and she was going to make good use of the sunny weather in India before the monsoon period started.

Sarika lay back on the recliner and closed her eyes. It was good to feel the heat of the sun against her skin, and she actually dozed until some hidden alarm warned her that she was no longer alone. Her long, silky lashes lifted to reveal wary tawny eyes, and her heart leapt into her throat at the sight of Sean O'Connor standing beside the recliner. His dark, furious gaze raked her from head to foot as she sat up abruptly, and she had a horrible feeling that her bikini had suddenly shrunk to half its size. What the devil was he doing at home so early in the afternoon?

'Ayah has enough to do without having to nurse you

if you have been foolish enough to roast yourself to a cinder,' his harsh voice lashed her, and her towelling robe was flung at her unceremoniously. 'Put that on, and get out of the sun.'

He turned on his heel and strode away, leaving Sarika to stare after him in a somewhat stunned silence until he had disappeared into the house. It was only than that her anger erupted. Who did he think he was to speak to her like that? How dared he treat her like an irresponsible child?

She put on her robe, and as she did so she felt a slight stinging sensation at her bare midriff where the towelling material brushed against her skin. She looked down, and her eyes widened at the pinkness she saw there. Sean was right, *damn him!* She had almost roasted herself!

Sarika entered the house with some trepidation, but Sean O'Connor was nowhere in sight as she went upstairs to her room to shower and change into something cool. It was not that Sean had returned home earlier than usual, she realised. It was she who had lingered beside the pool much longer than she had imagined. She had an hour to get herself ready for dinner, but she dreaded the thought of sitting down at the same table with Sean. Perhaps she could plead a headache and have a tray sent up to her room. No! Ayah would worry and think she was ill, and Sean was much too perceptive not to guess that she was trying to avoid him. That would only lead to more embarrassment, and she had been embarrassed sufficiently for the moment.

She put on a dress with a floral design printed on the pure, fine cotton, and she applied her make-up with care before she brushed her hair until it shone. With a touch of her favourite perfume behind her ears she was ready to go down and face the world. Or was she? Sean O'Connor's mocking features swam before her eyes, and suddenly she had butterflies in her stomach.

'Dammit, this is my home after all!' she muttered

angrily to herself. 'Why should I closet myself in my room because my parents saw fit to take in an insufferable lodger?'

She wrenched open the door and marched downstairs, to find that she would be dining alone with Ayah. Sean had received an urgent call, and he would not be back until much later that evening. The anti-climax was almost laughable, but Sarika doubted that Ayah would appreciate the joke, so she kept it to herself.

'I think I'd like to go into the office on Monday to start acquainting myself with the routine,' Sarika mentioned her decision to Ayah when they were lingering over their coffee.

'I won't allow it,' Ayah objected sternly. 'You have worked hard and you deserve a two-week break before you start working.'

'But I had a two-week break in Paris.'

'Maybe,' agreed Ayah, 'but it was not a restful holiday, and you need to rest before you start involving yourself in the business.'

Ayah was very persuasive, and Sarika eventually relented. Perhaps she did need a holiday, she told herself when tiredness made her go up to bed almost immediately after dinner.

Sarika awoke the following morning with that same feeling of uneasiness she had experienced the day before. She decided to spend the Saturday morning in town to do a bit of shopping and browsing. It would keep her occupied mentally and physically, and taking the bus instead of her car would be an added adventure.

She informed Ayah of her intentions and, despite Ayah's protestations that a Saturday was a bad day for shopping, she left the house shortly after breakfast and walked down to the bus stop. Five minutes later Sean O'Connor's Land Rover pulled up at the kerb beside her, and he leaned over to open the door on the passenger side.

'If you're going into the city, then I suggest you get

in,' he said tersely, and Sarika shrank inwardly from the idea of travelling into the city with him.

'I'd prefer to use the bus,' she said stubbornly.

'Get in!'

It was an order and, against her will, Sarika found herself obeying him. She got in beside him, and she had barely closed the door when he pulled away from the kerb and sped down the street.

Sean did not attempt to make conversation on the drive into town, and that suited Sarika perfectly. She sat staring out of the window at the passing landmarks, and tried to relax, but trying to relax with Sean was like trying to ride a tiger, for both were equally dangerous. The city streets were choked with traffic, and Sarika held her breath at times when she saw the small black and yellow taxis darting in and out among the larger vehicles.

'Where do you want to be dropped off?' Sean's voice sliced through the silence, and she glanced around a little wildly to see that they were approaching the Crawford Market.

'On this corner will do nicely, thank you.'

He pulled over sharply to the right and stopped the Land Rover. 'I'll pick you up here at twelve.'

'That won't be necessary,' she said abruptly, getting out and slamming the door. 'I'll take a bus.'

'Sarika!' He leaned across the front seat to speak to her through the open window, and his expression looked ominous. 'You will be here at twelve, and if I'm a bit late getting here through this traffic, you will wait. Is that understood?'

That note of authority in his voice warned her not to put up an argument, and she nodded mutely before she walked away from him. She cursed him silently for thinking he could order her about, but she soon forgot about Sean O'Connor when she literally had to elbow her way through the hordes of people on the street.

The market was crowded, and so were the shops. Ayah had been right, it was a bad day for coming in to town, but Sarika did not let that disturb her. She was in no hurry to get anywhere in particular, and she took her time browsing through the shops. The smell of incense was all around her and the babble of voices was almost deafening, but Sarika revelled in the atmosphere of this city she loved so much. Vendors lined the streets with their carts and, to Sarika, there was nothing strange about the vest and *dhoti* the men wore. Fifty per cent of the male population in India still wore the *dhoti*, a length of cotton material draped about the waist in a sash-like manner, pulled up between the legs, and then tucked into the waistband at the back. This was an integral part of India, and she hoped it would never change.

Sarika lingered over buying the few things she required, and she eventually stopped beside a cart in the street to buy a glass of sugar cane juice. She did so partly to quench her thirst, and partly to watch the fascinating procedure of coaxing the juice from the cane. The vendor pushed the stick of sugar cane through the roller part of the apparatus he had on his cart, and the juice dripped down on to a plate sprinkled with tiny pieces of ginger and lime. From there the juice ran down into a container of crushed ice. This procedure was repeated three times at least before all the juice had been squeezed out of the cane, and when Sarika finally sipped at her drink it was absolutely fabulous. With India's humid climate the drink made from sugar cane had been acclaimed as the ideal thirst quencher, and Sarika had found this to be true during her occasional trips into the city during her holidays in the past.

The hours had flown, and it was almost time to meet Sean. Sarika disposed of her paper cup and, clutching her parcels in her arms, shouldered her way through the milling throng to where Sean had ordered her to wait for him. Flushed and breathless, she arrived at the place where he had dropped her off barely seconds before the Land Rover pulled up next to her, and she was annoyed at being restricted in this way by a man like Sean O'Connor.

'There was really no need for you to go to all this trouble,' she said stiffly when she got into the Land Rover and slammed the door shut.

'Shut up!' he barked at her, and her anger rose by several degrees as he took her parcels from her and dumped them on the back seat.

'How dare you speak to me like that!'

'It's time someone put you in your place.'

'And you have decided you're the one to do it?' she demanded, thrust back against her seat with the force of the Land Rover pulling away from the kerb.

'I'm responsible for you in the absence of your parents.'

Sarika turned her head to stare incredulously at his dark, stern profile. 'I'm not a child, Mr O'Connor!'

'Then stop behaving like one!' he ordered sharply above the roar of the Land Rover. 'And you can skip the formal address. After the other night it can't be anything else but Sean, understand?'

'You don't have to shout, I can hear you perfectly well!' she informed him angrily. 'And I don't wish to be reminded of my first night at home.'

Sean did not reply to that, and Sarika would have maintained the stony silence between them if she had not seen him miss the turn-off to Malabar Hills.

'This isn't the way home.'

'I'm not taking you home,' came the terse reply. 'I'm taking you to lunch at the Taj Mahal Hotel.'

Sarika felt her chest tighten with something close to fear. 'Ayah is expecting me home for lunch.'

'No, she isn't,' he contradicted. 'I told her I'd be taking you somewhere to lunch with me.'

'You arranged this with Ayah without consulting me?' she demanded, her tawny eyes darting flames of incredulous anger at him.

'Why not?' He cast a brief, mocking glance in her direction. 'Don't you like my company?'

'No, I do not!' she exclaimed hotly.

'Well, that's too bad,' Sean shrugged his wide shoulders beneath the grey, lightweight jacket, 'because you're going to have to put up with my company for a while longer.'

Sarika lapsed into a mutinous silence. How *dared* he assume that she would want to have lunch with him, and how *dared* Ayah take it for granted that she would have accepted such an invitation! She was still smarting inwardly after what had happened between them on her first night in Bombay, and she was furious to think that her decision to stay out of his way had been thwarted in this manner.

The Taj Mahal Hotel's magnificent décor did nothing to soothe her temper, but Sean had at least chosen a table beside a window which gave her an excellent view of the pillared structure depicting the Gateway of India, and through it she had a clear glimpse of the sea which lay shimmering in the midday sun.

Sarika was too annoyed to be bothered with the menu, and she left it to Sean to order a light lunch for both of them. When the bar steward approached their table Sean turned to her for the first time and asked decisively, 'What would you like to drink?'

'A cold lemonade,' she said in an equally cold voice.

'A cold lemonade for the lady, and a whisky for me, please,' Sean ordered, and when the steward walked away he leaned back in his chair and studied her closely. 'Have you been here before?'

'A few times,' she answered abruptly, avoiding his eyes by staring out of the window.

'Not alone, I'm sure,' Sean mockingly attempted to induce conversation. 'All right, Sarika, let's have it!' he said at length when she maintained a stoic silence. 'Are you peeved because our little experiment the other night backfired on you?'

It was as if he had put a callous finger on a tender spot, and it felt as if a thousand volts shot through her. 'I haven't given it a thought.'

'Like *hell* you haven't!' he took up on her lie with a harsh laugh that made her steel herself before she allowed herself to look at him. 'You're a bad loser, and you still owe me an apology.'

'I owe you nothing!' she snapped moments before the steward appeared with their drinks.

'No girl slaps my face and gets away with it that easy,' murmured Sean threateningly the moment they were alone again, and his hand reached across the table unexpectedly to grip hers tightly. 'Apologise, Sarika, or I might be tempted to repeat the experiment right here.'

The sensuous curve of his chiselled mouth made her recall vividly the feel of his lips against her own, and his dark eyes issued a challenge she could not ignore.

'You're a——' The dangerous glitter in his eyes made her swallow her insulting words, and she finally admitted defeat when she murmured lamely, 'I apologise.'

There was a hateful ring of triumph in his soft, throaty laughter when he released her hand. 'That's a good girl.'

'Don't speak to me like that!' she snapped furiously.

'Like what?' he asked, taking a mouthful of whisky and swallowing it down before he raised a questioning eyebrow as he met her furious gaze across the table.

'As if I'm a child,' she elaborated stiffly.

'No, you're not a child.' The low pitch of his voice sent tremors racing along her taut nerves, and her insides trembled when his dark gaze took in every facet of her rigid features before trailing down to where her small, firm breasts were clearly defined beneath the close-fitting cotton bodice of her frock. Her body seemed to respond to his lingering gaze as if he had actually reached out across the table to touch her, and she felt a wave of heat surge from her throat into her face. 'You're a very beautiful woman.' The derisive twist to his mouth spoiled the compliment even before he added: 'But you're well aware of that, as I've said before.'

Those words were meant to sting, and they did. 'You made that sound like an insult.'

'I'm thirty-five, Sarika,' he inadvertently told her what she had been wondering about since their first meeting. 'I've known scores of very beautiful women, but I've also learnt that beautiful women mostly mean trouble. They're all spoilt and used to having their own way, and no woman is going to dictate to me what I should do with my life.'

So he was not married! She had wondered about this too, but the knowledge was followed by a disquieting sensation she could not explain to herself. Could it be the discovery that marriage did not feature in his plans for the future, or was it jealousy at the thought of all those unknown women? It was most certainly not the latter, she chastised herself severely, and it was with an anger directed at herself that she said icily, 'It doesn't interest me at all what you may or may not do with your life.'

'Are you campaigning for my attentions by trying to give the impression that you're different?' drawled Sean with a lazy, insolent smile, and the barometer of her fury rose to its limit.

'You're the most egotistical man I've ever met, and added to that you're also the most insufferable!' she spat out the words, and he leaned across the table towards her with something close to interest flickering in his dark glance.

'Did anyone ever tell you that your eyes are extraordinarily beautiful when you're angry?'

Sarika was momentarily stunned. It felt as if she had been thrown off a horse and had collided heavily with the earth, but she rallied swiftly. 'No,' she retorted sharply, 'and neither do I need you to tell me that!'

Sean laughed shortly, and the conversation fortunately ended there as their lunch was served.

She stared at the spiced chicken and salads on her plate. It looked extremely appetising, but she was not very hungry. She tried to relax, but she knew she dared not. To deal with someone like Sean O'Connor she needed all her wits about her, and for this reason she did not dare relax her guard.

Sarika made a pretence of eating while she studied him unobtrusively. Sean O'Connor was an authoritative and sometimes arrogant man who appeared to be accustomed to giving orders rather than taking them. She tried to imagine Sean in one of the junior posts at the Apex company, but she failed. He was not a junior; not in years and not in experience, and she once again had the strange notion that he was a man who would take command of a situation rather than accept commands from others. She was totally baffled and she longed to question him, but he had made it painfully clear that he disliked being questioned about himself. One thought led to another, and in the end she found herself trying to cope with that growing uneasiness which had plagued her since the day before.

'I had hoped I would have heard from my parents by now,' she found herself voicing her thoughts. 'Have they perhaps been in contact with someone at the office?'

'If we'd heard from them I would have told you.' He pushed his plate aside and gestured to the waiter to bring their tea before he settled back in his chair and glanced at her mockingly. 'Don't tell me you're worried about them?'

'I . . . no, not really. It's just that I . . .' She pulled herself together sharply and put down her knife and fork to gesture helplessly with her slender hands. 'Oh, I can't explain it, but I have this uneasy feeling, and I can't seem to shake it off.'

She held her breath, expecting him to mock her, but his rugged features remained impassive for once. 'They can take care of themselves.'

'Yes, I'm sure they can,' she admitted reluctantly, vaguely ashamed of having admitted her fears to someone like Sean O'Connor who seemed to have little or no opinion of her at all.

She left the rest of her food untouched and settled for her cup of tea. Sean's glance flicked towards the plate which had barely been touched and his mouth tightened, but, surprisingly, he said nothing. He questioned her instead about her studies in England, and she answered him automatically. They discussed certain aspects of architecture, and meeting him on the same level for the first time was an enjoyable and enlightening experience. His ideas were not staid as she had imagined they might be, but modern like her own. She also found that they agreed on several things, and that made a welcome change from the antagonism which had been sparked off between them from the moment they had met.

The drive back to her home was not as unpleasant as she had thought it might be. They did not talk much, but the silence between them was not uncomfortable and, when they arrived at the house, she did not object to being instructed to take herself and her parcels into the house while Sean garaged the Land Rover.

Sarika felt strangely calm. It was, she realised afterwards, that same calmness one often encountered directly before a savage storm erupted. She stepped into the cool, quiet entrance hall with its marble floor, and the telephone started ringing almost as if it had waited for that moment when she would arrive.

She dropped her parcels on to the chair beside the telephone table and lifted the receiver to her ear. She gave her name, but there was some disturbance at the other end of the line before an unfamiliar voice demanded, 'Who is speaking, please?'

'Sarika Maynesfield,' she repeated her name, still enveloped by that strange cloak of calmness.

'Miss Maynesfield, this is Sergeant Singh of the Bombay Police,' the voice informed her, and her stomach lurched sickeningly.

'What can I do for you, Sergeant Singh?' The line went ominously silent and, thinking they might have been cut off, she said in a raised voice, 'Hello? Hello, can you hear me? Are you still there?'

Sergeant Singh coughed and cleared his throat, indicating that he was still very much at the other end of the line, then he started speaking in a strangely sombre voice. 'Miss Maynesfield, I am afraid I have unpleasant news to pass on to you.'

Again the line went silent, and Sarika prompted him frantically. 'What is the matter, Sergeant Singh? What has happened?'

'I am afraid that the yacht your parents were sailing on has disappeared,' came the dreaded, crushing reply. 'The Karachi port officials received a distress signal this morning, but the reception was very bad, and they have been unable to pinpoint the location of the yacht. A sea and air rescue team is out searching for them, but as yet their search has been unsuccessful.'

Sarika leaned heavily against the ornate marble telephone stand with the decorative mirror above it, and an icy numbness took possession of her as she stared blankly at the reflection of her stark white features. She knew now the reason for her uneasiness, but that did not make this horrifying news any less difficult to accept.

CHAPTER FOUR

SEAN's rugged face appeared in the mirror beside Sarika's. She tried to speak to him, her lips moved, but she could not make a sound.

'Sarika, what's the matter? Why are you——'

'Hello! Hello, can you hear me, Miss Maynesfield?'

Sergeant Singh's voice came clearly from the receiver that dangled from her limp fingers, and Sean snatched the receiver from Sarika's hand. 'Hello, this is Sean O'Connor.'

Sarika stepped away from the table and leaned weakly against the wall while Sean spoke to the Sergeant. Ayah came bustling towards them from the direction of the kitchen. She took one look at Sarika's white face, and quickened her pace.

'What is going on?' Ayah demanded just as Sean replaced the receiver on its cradle. 'Tell me what has happened?'

'Reg Parker's yacht seems to have disappeared after sending out a distress signal this morning,' explained Sean. 'The Karachi port officials say there's a heavy storm raging up their way, and they couldn't get a bearing on the yacht's position at the time because the connection was severed. They're searching a wide radius in the hope of finding survivors, and the port officials have alerted all possible ships in the vicinity to be on the look-out for the yacht.'

'My poor Sarika,' Ayah crooned, her own face whitening with shock and grief as she took Sarika's arm and led her towards the living-room. 'My poor *beti*!'

Sarika walked like someone in a trance. At that moment she could feel nothing except that dreadful coldness as if she had been thrust into a bath filled with ice cubes. Ayah helped her into a chair, and she sat there staring straight ahead of her while Ayah fussed and crooned endearments.

'Drink this, it will make you feel better,' Sean's gravelly voice intruded into Sarika's numb world, and a glass of amber liquid was thrust into her line of vision. She shook her head in silent refusal, but he placed the glass in her hand, and held it there with his own as he raised it to her lips. 'Drink it!' he barked sternly.

Her nose wrinkled with distaste when she realised it was brandy, but she sipped it obediently, and as the welcoming warmth surged through her cold body, Sean removed his hand from about hers and left her to drink the brandy on her own. She could not drink more than half the amount he had poured for her, but he seemed satisfied when she handed the glass back to him.

'They're not coming back,' she said at last in a husky, anguished voice. 'They're not coming back, I know it!'

'Sarika, listen to me,' Sean intruded on Ayah's tender ministrations to lean over Sarika and grip her shoulders firmly. 'There's no cause yet to think the worst. The area the authorities have to search is vast, and there's every chance that Dave and Cara may still be found alive.'

'I know they won't be coming back,' Sarika insisted in a wooden voice. 'They're dead . . . I feel it!'

Ayah muttered something unintelligible as Sean released Sarika with an exasperated exclamation on his lips. 'I suggest you take her up to her room, Ayah, and make her lie down,' he instructed tersely. 'I have a few phone calls to make, but I'll look in later.'

'Come with me, *pyaari*,' murmured Ayah sympathetically as Sean strode out of the living-room. 'I will take care of you.'

Sarika wanted to cry as Ayah led her across the hall and up the stairs to her room, but the tears would not come. They were locked inside her like a heavy, leaden ache behind a steel door, and she herself had long since thrown away the key. She did not want to get into bed.

She ignored Ayah's pleas and began to pace the floor with her arms wrapped about herself.

She was shaking inside when Sean finally walked into her room. His glance lingered for a moment on her white face with the haunted eyes, then he turned to Ayah. 'I've called the doctor, and he'll be here as soon as he can make it, but Sarika should be lying down.'

'I don't want to lie down, and I don't need a doctor!' Saraika protested, her teeth chattering as that icy coldness surged through her again.

'You're suffering from shock,' argued Sean with a calmness that suddenly infuriated her, and she turned on him with her eyes blazing.

'I don't need a doctor!'

'Calm down, *beti*,' Ayah murmured soothingly, her hands smoothing Sarika's honey-blonde hair away from her white face. 'Sean is only doing what he considers is best for you.'

'Best for me?' Sarika wanted to shout out in anguish. 'How does he know what's best for me?' The words, however, never left her lips. The room began to spin crazily, and the darkness of night seemed to descend upon her. She tried to fight it off, but it was too strong for her, and the last thing she remembered was the curious sensation that the floor was lifting to collide with her.

Sarika eventually surfaced sufficiently to realise that someone had undressed her and put her to bed, and she could only pray that it had been Ayah. Dr Banerjee was sitting next to her on the bed, and he was asking her questions while he examined her. She was answering him, but she had no clear knowledge of what she was actually saying. She felt the sting of a needle being jabbed into her arm, and then she knew no more until she awoke to a silence which was disturbed seconds later by the creaking of a chair.

She turned her head against the pillow in the dimly lit room, and her glance collided with Sean's dark eyes. He was sitting in the chair beside her bed and, in the grip of sudden terror, she sat up abruptly and clutched the sheets about her. What was he doing in her bedroom? And then she recalled all the terrible details of what had occurred that day.

'What time is it?' she asked, still feeling slightly drugged as she pushed her fingers through her tumbled hair.

'It's two-thirty in the morning,' Sean informed her after consulting his watch, and in the bedside light his rugged features took on a haggard look.

'What are you doing here in my room?' she demanded, her eyes widening at the discovery that Dr Banerjee's injection had made her sleep for hours.

'Ayah and I have been taking turns to sit with you.'

She felt embarrassed at the thought that he had been sitting there beside her bed while she was sleeping, but from the partly drugged recesses of her mind came an urgent query. 'Has there been any further news?'

'None.'

'They won't find them, you know,' she said with a fatalistic conviction which she could not explain.

Sean stared at her oddly for a moment, then he got up and walked across to the low table between the padded chairs. 'Ayah left soup in a flask for you.'

'I don't want anything.'

'You hardly touched your lunch, and you slept through dinner.' She could hear him pouring something into a cup, then he turned and walked towards the bed with a firm tread. 'You must keep your strength up, so drink this soup.'

Strong fingers dislodged her hand from the sheets she clutched beneath her chin, and the cup of soup was placed in it. Sarika stared a long way up into that unrelenting face, and she simply did not have the strength to argue.

'I don't know why I let you bully me this way,' she muttered angrily, sipping at the hot liquid and finding it extremely tasty.

'At the moment you're incapable of taking care of yourself, so someone has to take charge.'

Sarika digested this slowly, and studied him speculatively over the rim of her mug when he resumed his seat. 'You're used to taking charge, aren't you,' she said at length. 'You're accustomed to being in a position of authority.'

Sean raised a sardonic eyebrow. 'What makes you say that?'

'It's just a feeling I have, and it makes me wonder why someone like yourself would want to work for my father.' She paled suddenly as the nightmare of the situation sent a new wave of coldness through her. 'I don't suppose they will continue the search in the dark.'

'They'll start again first thing in the morning.'

Sarika swallowed convulsively and tried to concentrate on drinking her soup, but her glance lingered on Sean. His features looked grim and drawn, and a shadowy growth of beard was beginning to show along the side of his jaw.

'Go to bed, Sean, you look exhausted.'

A hint of a smile touched his stern mouth. 'Are you trying to take charge of me now?'

'None of this need really concern you,' she tried to explain. 'They're my parents, and you merely work for my father.'

There was an odd little silence that filled her with uneasiness before he said harshly, 'My concern goes far deeper than you may realise at this moment, so don't attempt to shut me out, Sarika.'

She felt like a child who had been rapped once again over the knuckles, and lowered her gaze apologetically. 'I didn't intend my remark to sound rude.'

'Didn't you?' he mocked her, and his mockery was something she could not tolerate at that moment.

'Oh, please just go and leave me alone!' she begged huskily, lowering her head so that her hair fell forward to veil her quivering lips.

'I'll go, but I'll ask Ayah to come here to you.'

Sarika opened her mouth to protest, but he had gone, and she sat there in her silent, suddenly empty room, nursing her mug of soup between her trembling hands. She tried to drink her soup, but for some inexplicable reason it had become tasteless, and she was turning to place the mug on the bedside cupboard when Ayah walked into the room and closed the door behind her.

'Beti?' she enquired anxiously as she approached the bed, and all Sarika's fears suddenly leapt to the fore.

'Ayah!' she croaked. 'Oh, Ayah, what if they don't come back?'

'Then it is something we must accept, Sarika,' came the calm reply, but Sarika stubbornly refused to surrender to such logic.

'I shall never accept it!' she cried huskily, clinging to her somewhat childish hopes and dreams. 'There was so much I still wanted to do; so much I still hoped for. If they don't come back I shall never have the opportunity to tell them how much I loved them, and I'll never know if they loved me.'

'Pyaari,' crooned Ayah, stroking the heavy strands of hair away from Sarika's white, anguished face with gentle hands. 'Life is not always kind that way. My husband died before I could tell him I loved him, and as a result of his accident I lost the child I was carrying before I could hold it in my arms. I came to your parents a broken young woman who had to learn to accept what fate had dealt me, and that is why, when you were born, I took you to my heart as my own. You were such a pretty little thing, and Cara *bhenji* did me the honour of letting me name you. Sarika was the name I chose for you, and Cara *bhenji* placed you in my care from that very first day you opened your eyes to this sometimes cruel world.' There were tears in Ayah's dark brown eyes when she framed Sarika's face with her hands. 'Sarika, *pyaari,* God takes away, but he also gives back in ways that are wonderful, and, as he gave me you, he will also give to you someone to love and someone who will love you.'

Sarika felt something snap inside her; she felt her shoulders begin to shake, and then she was crying all over Ayah's white sari. The arms that held her were comforting and familiar, and once the tears had started Sarika could not stop them. They poured down her cheeks as if a dam inside her was overflowing, and Ayah, in her wisdom, did not attempt to check these great, choking tears that tore through Sarika's slender body.

'Oh, Ayah, Ayah!' Sarika sobbed at length against a scented shoulder which had become damp with her tears. 'What would I have done all these years without you?'

Ayah did not answer her. She merely rocked her in her arms and crooned those familiar endearments which had always succeeded in soothing Sarika through her childhood.

Sarika leaned back against the pillows with an exhausted sigh when the emotional storm had abated, and Ayah pulled the sheets up over her. 'Go to sleep, Sarika. Tomorrow will be a long day for you, and you must preserve your strength.'

Sarika did succeed in going to sleep again, and this time it was a natural, self-induced sleep from which she did not awaken until seven o'clock the Sunday morning. She leapt out of bed, bathed and dressed herself in navy cotton slacks and a white sleeveless blouse, and was seated at the breakfast table when Sean walked in. His jaw was clean-shaven, but his features still bore that grim expression she had seen in the early hours of the morning.

'Good morning,' he said abruptly, helping himself to bacon and eggs. 'I trust you slept again after I left your room last night . . . or rather this morning?'

'I slept well, thank you,' she murmured, feeling vaguely ashamed at making such a confession when he bore the look of a man who had stayed awake all night. 'Did you sleep?'

'No,' he confirmed her suspicions. 'I sat up all night

in case the police had some news to telephone through to us.'

'There wasn't any news, was there?' she asked, holding her breath.

'None,' he answered abruptly, attacking his breakfast with a vigour she envied while she sat struggling to force down a slice of toast and coffee.

Ayah brought in a fresh pot of coffee for Sean, and some minutes later he got up from the table with the announcement, 'I'm going down to the police station to find out what's going on, and if there isn't something I could do.'

'I'm coming with you!' Sarika stopped him before he reached the door and, dabbing at her mouth with the table napkin, she got up from the table and said a hasty goodbye to Ayah before she followed Sean out of the house.

They did not speak to each other on the way to the police station. Sean sat staring grimly ahead of him while Sarika was trying to cope with her own thoughts. Her mind flitted over the past in an effort to recall one loving gesture from her parents. They had been devoted to each other, there was no doubt in her mind about that, but their devotion had never spilled over on to her. There had been a few occasions when they had tagged her along to a function as an adornment they could display to their friends, but the novelty had worn off as swiftly as it had begun. None of this had altered her feelings for her parents. She had loved them, and she had always believed that they loved her, but no verbal confirmation of their feelings had ever passed between them. There had never been a closeness between them such as the closeness that existed between Ayah and herself, and Sarika felt choked with sadness at the thought.

Sean turned in at the police station some minutes later and parked his Land Rover close to the entrance. Sarika shivered despite the warmth of the sun on her skin, and she welcomed the protective strength of

Sean's hand beneath her elbow when they entered the building.

'I want to speak to Sergeant Singh,' Sean said authoritatively to the young policeman who had leapt to attention behind the counter. 'Tell him it's urgent.'

'May I have your name, please?' the young Indian man asked politely, a hint of awe in his eyes when he looked up at Sean.

'O'Connor,' Sean aswered abruptly. 'Sean O'Connor.'

The policeman stepped out from behind the counter and disappeared so quickly that Sarika did not notice which direction he had taken. She cast a swift, anxious glance up at Sean, and a faintly reassuring smile touched his mouth, but Sarika was too tense to relax. The young policeman appeared moments later, and she felt her facial muscles go rigid with nerves.

'Sergeant Singh will see you now,' he announced. 'If you will come this way, please.'

He led the way down a long, gloomy passage to a door on the right which stood slightly ajar, and he stepped aside respectfully as he gestured them to enter.

The Sergeant was a short, bulky man, and he rose behind his desk when they entered his office. 'Good morning, Mr O'Connor . . . Miss Maynesfield . . . please take a seat.'

'What news do you have for us?' Sean asked the moment they sat facing the sergeant across the wide desk.

'I am afraid that as yet I have no positive information to pass on to you,' Sergeant Singh answered regretfully. 'The Karachi police are still investigating the disappearance of the yacht, and the authorities have renewed their sea and air search, but other than that I cannot tell you anything.'

'A yacht the size of Reg Parker's can't simply disappear without trace,' Sean argued harshly, voicing Sarika's own panic-stricken thoughts.

'I am aware of that,' the Sergeant replied calmly, 'but

in a storm such as the one that lashed the Pakistani coast, anything could have happened. They could have drifted off their course, and there is no telling where their exact location might have been at the time they sent out their distress signal.' His glance shifted to Sarika's white, pinched face, and his expression was at once sympathetic. 'I am sorry, Miss Maynesfield. I know how painful this must be to you, and I can understand your anxiety.'

'Isn't there anything one can do to speed up the search?' Sean questioned the man behind the desk. 'Apex has a helicopter which could be of use.'

'I assure you, Mr O'Connor, that everything possible is being done at this moment to find the yacht as well as the people on board,' the Sergeant replied. 'To interfere might lengthen the procedure, so my suggestion is that you leave the matter in the hands of the proper authorities.'

'You will let us know the moment you have any news?' Sarika interrupted the tense little silence which had followed the Sergeant's statement, and the man nodded emphatically.

'I will see to it that you are notified immediately.'

Sean thanked the man abruptly and, taking Sarika by the arm, he ushered her out of the office, down the gloomy passage, and out of the building to where he had parked his Land Rover.

'What do we do now?' asked Sarika when Sean got in beside her.

'We wait!' came the terse reply, and, when he saw the expression that flitted across her face, he added harshly, '*Dammit*, Sarika, there's nothing else we can do!'

They waited throughout that Sunday for news. Sean slept in the study that night in order to hear the telephone, and he did not go to the office on the Monday morning. They were having tea out on the terrace when the telephone rang shrilly in the hall, and both Sarika and Sean leapt to their feet to answer it, but Sean reached it first.

'Sean O'Connor,' he said abruptly into the mouthpiece.

His dark eyes met Sarika's while he listened to the voice at the other end, and Sarika could feel the perspiration breaking out on her forehead. She stood like a statue except for the twitching of a nerve at the corner of her generous mouth, and it seemed like an eternity before Sean replaced the receiver on its cradle.

'What have you heard? Have they found them?' Her voice sounded shrill in the spacious hall. 'For God's sake, tell me!'

'Control yourself, Sarika!' She stood quiveringly tense beneath the hands that gripped her shoulders, and she was vaguely aware of Ayah hovering somewhere in the background while Sean spoke to her in a lowered voice. 'They've located the yacht. It was wrecked on the rocks, and they've picked up the occupants along the coast about ten miles south of Karachi.'

'They're dead, aren't they!' she said through stiff lips.

'I'm afraid so.'

Sarika was aware of an overpowering dizziness, and she collapsed against Sean's wide chest as that dark curtain shifted over her mind.

It was some time later that Sarika regained consciousness. She was lying on her bed with Ayah seated beside her, and she had no idea how she had got there, or why she was lying there.

'You gave us such a fright, Sarika,' Ayah frowned at her worriedly. 'Sean carried you up here, and the doctor has just left after seeing you.'

The stark reality of what had occurred down in the hall suddenly washed over her, and Sarika felt a numb pain take hold of her as if her chest had been clamped in a vice.

'Sean?' she queried in a whisper, and Ayah explained in a hushed voice.

'Sean has taken the company helicopter and is at this

moment flying to Karachi with Sergeant Singh to make a positive identification of the bodies.'

Sarika winced visibly. It sounded horrible! Her parents had been robbed of their identities, and now they were simply *bodies*. She had had a premonition that something was going to happen. When the news of the yacht's disappearance came through she had known somehow that she would never see them again, but the knowledge that they were dead was so frighteningly final that it left her numb and dazed with the horror of it.

'If you don't mind, Ayah, I would like to be left alone for a while.'

Ayah nodded understandingly. 'If you need me, *pyaari*, you know you only have to call.'

The silence and the emptiness in the room after Ayah had left was symbolic of the silent void left by the death of her parents, and Sarika felt herself shrinking mentally beneath a red mist of pain. She got up and walked across to the window to stare blindly down into the sunlit garden, then her very heartbeat seemed to stop as a strange calmness engulfed her. It was as if she had gone into a place of seclusion where nothing could touch her. There was no pain, only a deadly calmness which seemed to leave no room for thought.

Sarika went through the motions of living during the next few days, but she did so in a trance-like state. She knew that her parents' bodies had been flown back to Bombay, she was aware of Sean discussing the funeral arrangements with her, and she knew she had answered him, but nothing seemed to strike a chord of emotion inside her. The funeral had been arranged for the Thursday and, flanked by Sean and Ayah, Sarika had stood dry-eyed and pale beside the graves. Sean had driven them home afterwards in his Land Rover, and Sarika had gone up to her room immediately afterwards to sit in front of the window with eyes that saw nothing, and a heart that felt even less.

Ayah brought a light lunch on a tray up to Sarika's

room, but she did not touch it, and Ayah shook her head despairingly when she removed the tray an hour later.

'Sarika,' Ayah spoke her name quietly when she entered her room again much later that afternoon, 'Jaishree is here to see you.'

The mention of her friend's name failed to bring so much as a flicker of interest to Sarika's eyes. 'I don't want to see anyone at the moment.'

'But, Sarika——' Ayah broke off abruptly and gestured helplessly with her hands before she walked out of the room and closed the door softly behind her.

The hours passed, but it could have been days, for Sarika had no conception of time while she sat there staring straight ahead of her with a blank expression in her eyes. Her dinner that evening was once again brought to her room on a tray, and Ayah sternly ordered her to eat it. Sarika obeyed her like a child with no will of its own, but the tastefully prepared meal refused to go down, and she left it practically untouched.

'Sarika, *pyaari*, you cannot shut us out like this,' Ayah complained gently when she came up later that evening to fetch the tray. 'You cannot lock yourself away somewhere in a world where no one can reach you. The death of your parents has touched us all very deeply, but if we stand together it is something we will overcome.'

Ayah's words seemed to penetrate that invisible wall behind which Sarika had sought refuge, and she flinched visibly. 'Please, Ayah, I don't wish to discuss it!'

'*Beti*,' the woman shook her head gravely, 'you are making a terrible mistake.'

She picked up the tray and walked out of the room without saying another word, and when the door closed behind her, Sarika shrank back into that self-made world of conscious oblivion.

Sarika was not aware of how much time had elapsed

before she became aware of someone else in the room with her. Something akin to fear intruded into her world of calm, and she turned her head sharply. Sean, grim and dark, was leaning with his back against her closed door, and his arms were crossed over his wide chest. His black shirt was unbuttoned almost to his waist, and a silver medallion on a chain nestled among the dark chest hair. The raw masculinity of his appearance seemed to trigger off something inside her which she could not control, and she rose abruptly from her chair to face him.

'I didn't hear you knocking!' she accused sharply.

'I didn't knock.'

His effrontery kindled a flame of anger inside her. 'You may behave as if this entire house belongs to you, but this happens to be my room, so will you please get out!'

'Not until we've talked,' he said, pushing himself away from the door and dropping his arms to his sides as he approached her.

'I don't want to talk to you!' she almost shouted at him as she backed against the chair, and she clutched at it to steady herself.

'Pull yourself together, Sarika!' he ordered harshly. 'It's time you faced up to the reality that your parents are dead. They're never coming back, but you're still alive, and you have to go on living!'

'Shut up, do you hear me!' she hissed up at him with a fury that had erupted from some hidden part of her. 'Shut up!'

'I suggest you calm yourself.'

'I am calm!' The note of hysteria in her voice belied that statement. 'Just get out of my room and leave me alone! I don't want to talk to you, or to anyone else!'

'Sarika!'

'Get out!'

His dark gaze flicked over her disparagingly. 'Well, I came here hoping to get some sort of reaction from you, and I guess this is better than nothing.'

'Oh, why can't you leave me alone!' she cried, her insides starting to shake as if the foundations were beginning to shudder beneath her feet.

'I can't leave you alone because *someone* has to drum some sense into your silly little head,' came the terse reply. 'Ayah has attempted to do so with kindness and she's failed, but I don't intend to be kind, and I don't intend to fail.'

His arrogant, self-assured manner was like putting a match to an inflammable object, and her fury erupted with a violence that stormed through her. 'I hate you, Sean O'Connor!' she shouted at him. 'I hate you!'

'You can't kick against fate, and you're going to hate me a whole lot more before I'm finished with you,' he laughed, and his laughter seemed to shatter the last fragment of her control.

Sarika leapt at him, her hands raised and her fingers curled to rake his face with her nails, but fingers of steel were clamped about her wrists, and her arms were pinned helplessly behind her back. She fought like a tigress, but every movement simply made her increasingly aware of his hard male body aginst her own, and tears of frustration finally filled her eyes. It was as if someone had suddenly turned the key in a rusted lock, and there was nothing she could do to stop the tears that flowed down her pale cheeks. She slumped against Sean's big, strong body, and he released her wrists to cradle her in his arms with her face buried against his broad chest.

'That's it, honey,' he murmured, his hand stroking her hair gently. 'Crying is the best therapy for you at this moment.'

His unexpected gentleness and understanding was her undoing, and she wept in his arms until she was drained almost of all emotion. She was lifted in his strong arms when her tears subsided, and he carried her across the room to lower her on to her bed.

'Don't leave me!' Her voice was hoarse and

frightened, and she clutched at his arms when it seemed as if he was going to move away from her. 'Please, Sean, don't leave me yet!'

'I'll stay for as long as you need me, honey,' he said gravely as he seated himself on the bed beside her and, reassured, she relaxed against the pillows.

'Why do you call me honey?' she asked, wiping the last traces of her tears from her red, puffy eyes with a damp, lacy handkerchief.

'I don't know,' he smiled faintly, stretching out a hand to run his fingers through her silky hair where it trailed across her shoulder. 'Perhaps it's the colour of your hair. It reminds me of the honey I used to steal as a child in the forest near my home.'

He seemed so incredibly human and so very approachable at that moment that she risked questioning him about himself. 'Your surname is Irish, but you don't have the looks of the Irish. Why is that?'

'My father was an Irishman who emigrated to America, but my mother was Mexican.'

'That explains it, then,' she murmured, taking in his dark, brooding appearance.

'Explains what?' he demanded mockingly.

'Your eyes,' she said without hesitation, and with a certain amount of bravado. 'They're so dark they're almost black, and they seem to have a perpetual fire smouldering in them. Does your mother have a fiery Latin nature?'

'I believe she did,' he smiled briefly, curling his fingers deeper into her lustrous hair. 'She died when I was eight.'

'I'm sorry,' she whispered, his face becoming a blur through the tears that sprang so readily now to her eyes.

'Don't cry for me, Sarika,' he said, that gravelly note in his voice deepening. 'I was too young at the time to really understand what had happened, and I subsequently adapted easily to my loss.'

'Your father?' she continued to question him while

she did her best to blink away her tears. 'Is he still alive?'

'No,' he answered gravely. 'He suffered a severe stroke four years ago.'

'Oh!' she croaked, and now she could not check the tears that spilled on to her cheeks.

'You'd better use this,' instructed Sean, removing her sodden handkerchief from her fingers and giving her his own.

'I don't know what's the matter with me,' she said at length when she had succeeded in controlling herself. 'I haven't cried like this in ages.'

'It's never good to bottle up one's emotions, Sarika.'

'I suppose you're right,' she sighed, blowing her nose into the expensive white cotton handkerchief, and mopping up the last of her tears.

'Feeling better?' he smiled at her without his usual mockery, and an answering smile plucked at the corners of her wide, quivering mouth.

'Yes, thank you,' she said. 'I'll be all right now.'

His fingers brushed lightly against her cheek and, for a moment, his smouldering eyes burned down into hers in a way that made her heart skip a beat. His mood changed abruptly, and he stood up and walked away from her. 'I suggest you get undressed and get into bed.'

'Sean . . .' He stood with his hand resting on the brass handle of the door, and his features had settled back into its usual harsh mask. 'Would you ask Ayah to come up here, please?'

He nodded, and then she was alone and left to wonder what had brought about the sudden change in him. He had come very close to showing her a little kindness, but his manner and his expression had altered so swiftly that she could almost believe she had imagined it. His handkerchief was real, however, and she was still clutching it to her trembling lips when Ayah entered her room and walked towards the bed.

'You wanted me, Sarika?' she smiled despite the concern still mirrored in her dark eyes.

'Oh, Ayah!' Lapsing into a renewed bout of tears, she held out her arms to this woman who had always been more than a nanny to her. 'I want to apologise for being so awful to you.'

'An apology is not necessary, *pyaari*,' Ayah assured her while they embraced. 'I know how you are suffering, and I understand better than anyone else the reason for it.'

'I'm so glad I still have you,' Sarika managed to smile through her tears when they held each other at arm's length.

'Get undressed and go to sleep, Sarika,' Ayah instructed gently, taking Sean's handkerchief and wiping away Sarika's tears. 'Tomorrow might be a day with problems of its own, and you will need the strength to cope with it.'

Sarika did not think to question Ayah's statement, but she had cause to remember it the following afternoon.

CHAPTER FIVE

On the Friday morning Sarika and Ayah received a summons from the attorney's office. They had to see a Mr Webster at two-thirty that afternoon for the reading of her father's will. Sarika had no intention of going into mourning, but Ayah insisted that she wear a sombre grey linen suit for the occasion, while Ayah herself was dressed in her usual white sari with a touch of grey in it.

'I'm not looking forward to this,' Sarika confessed, seated behind the wheel of her Mercedes sports for the first time since her return to Bombay.

'It is not always pleasant,' Ayah agreed, 'but it is necessary.'

Necessary! The word ricocheted through Sarika's mind. The death of her parents had not been necessary. If they had still been alive, then none of this would have been *necessary*!

Sarika drove past the shrine to three faiths which was in the middle of a traffic island in the city. On the one side was a white plaster cross of Christ; on another, a small stone image of the elephant-trunked Ganesh, the Hindu god of good fortune; and on a third, a small concrete altar on which worshippers placed the Koran when they prayed to Allah. It was one of Sarika's favourite places, and so symbolic of the India of today, but on this occasion she gave it no more than a casual glance. Her mind was filled with sombre, angry thoughts of the blow fate had dealt her, and she wondered why she had this nagging suspicion that fate had not yet finished with her.

Sean was leaning against his Land Rover smoking a cheroot when they arrived at the building which housed the offices of Webster and Bramley, Attorneys at Law.

His presence did not somehow surprise Sarika, but her heart did seem to negotiate an uncomfortable somersault when she saw him crush his cheroot beneath the heel of his expensive shoe. There was something quite savage about the action, and she sensed that same savagery in his manner when he came striding towards them.

Flanked once again by Sean and Ayah, Sarika entered the modern, air-conditioned building. They took the lift up to the third floor and were ushered, without delay, into the attorney's modernly furnished office. Mr Webster, a slender man with greying hair, stepped from behind his deesk to welcome them.

'I'm sorry we have to meet under these unfortunate circumstances,' he said when he clasped Sarika's hand briefly, then he gestured towards the chairs which had been arranged around his desk. 'Won't you all please take a seat.'

Sarika seated herself between Ayah and Sean, and locked her hands tightly in her lap. A sealed envelope was taken from the safe, and only then did the attorney seat himself behind his desk. The genuine leather-upholstered chair creaked loudly in the silent room, and the attorney's watery grey eyes once again settled on Sarika's white face.

'Miss Maynesfield, I have here your parents' last will and testament, which was drawn up six months ago in this office,' he explained, his bony fingers tapping the large brown envelope on the blotter in front of him. 'With your permission I would like to disclose its contents.'

With your permission! What would happen if she withheld her permission? For one frightening moment she actually toyed with the idea before she said: 'Please go ahead, Mr Webster.'

The attorney put on his horn-rimmed spectacles and broke the seal on the envelope. It was too late now to change her mind, Sarika thought crazily, then the attorney's emotionless voice shut out every other thought from her mind.

Ayah would inherit a substantial amount from the estate with which she could live comfortably for the rest of her life, and Sarika was very happy about this, but, as the attorney continued speaking, she found herself becoming increasingly confused.

'I'm afraid I don't understand,' she said eventually when the attorney's voice lapsed into silence. 'The will states that I inherit forty-nine per cent of the shares in the Apex Company. May I know what's happened to the rest of the shares, and why is there no mention of my parents' home?'

The eyes behind the horn-rimmed spectacles darted a glance at Sean before they settled again on Sarika. 'The greater portion of the shares, as well as the house, belongs to Mr O'Connor, and has done so for the past six months.'

It felt to Sarika as if someone had delivered a vicious blow to her midriff, and she sat there literally gasping for air like a fish out of water. 'No!' she gasped at length, turning in her chair to stare at Sean with a stunned expression in her eyes. 'No, I don't believe it!'

'Would you leave us alone for a few minutes?' Sean's features were savagely grim when he spoke to the attorney and directed his gaze beyond Sarika. 'Ayah?'

Mr Webster and Ayah left the office without Sarika actually being aware that they had done so. She was staring at Sean and desperately trying to assimilate the news she had received.

'I don't believe it!' She shook her head, her hair a deep gold as it danced about her shoulders in the shaft of sunlight that fell across the desk.

'Your father had been speculating on the stock market, and he suffered some heavy losses a year ago. The house was subsequently heavily mortgaged, but he needed a lot more money, and he needed it fast,' Sean explained, his voice low and harsh in the silent room. 'I was investigating the possibility of starting a business here in Bombay when your father approached me, so I bought myself into your father's company, and took over the majority of the shares. It was your father's intention to retire eventually and buy himself a cottage somewhere along the coast. When he talked of selling the house I bought it as it stands on the understanding that Dave and Cara stayed on until they found something suitable.'

Was this why her father had refused to finance her boutique? *No*, she shrugged off the thought, *he had always thought only of himself!* Sarika rose slowly to her feet, but she had to clutch at the desk the next instant when the floor seemed to heave beneath her. 'Why was I never told?'

'Your father was going to do that.' Sean got up and walked to the window with that same savagery in his movements which she had witnessed earlier. 'Unfortunately he left it too late.'

'*You* could have told me,' she accused, the numbness dispersing to leave her face to face with the humiliating truth.

'I wanted to tell you last night, but I figured you'd had enough for one day,' he said, turning to face her with his jaw thrust out angrily, and his eyes watchful.

Sarika stood there staring at him, her hands clutching her handbag so tightly that her knuckles shone white through the skin. Her secure, familiar world had suddenly crumbled about her to leave her in utter chaos. Her mind was grasping frantically for something to cling to, but everything had suddenly disintegrated.

'What a fool you must think me, accusing you of taking liberties in my father's home, while all the time it was I . . .' Sarika could not continue as a fiery wave of humiliation engulfed her. All she could hear was her own voice making scathing remarks about Sean's presence in what she had believed to be her home, and shame sent crimson flags into her white face. 'Oh, God!' she groaned and, unable to face Sean a moment longer, she turned and fled from the attorney's office before anyone could stop her.

Sarika selfishly thought of no one but herself at that

moment as she ran out of the building and got into her car. She had to get away; she had to think, but most of all she had to get away from Sean O'Connor.

She had no idea where she had driven to; she could have gone in circles for all she knew, but she came to her senses two hours later to find herself approaching the shrine to three faiths, and there was one thought firmly lodged in her otherwise chaotic mind. She could not stay in that house knowing that it belonged to Sean!

The sun was beginning to set when Sarika finally arrived at the house and garaged her car. She walked round to the front of the house and paused for a moment to stare up at the pillared mansion. This had been her home, and she had considered Sean an intruder, but the tables had turned. The house belonged to Sean, and *she* was the intruder. It was a thought she could not bear to linger on and, brushing it aside, she ran lightly up the steps.

'Where the hell have you been?' Sean's voice thundered at her when she entered the hall, and she spun round to see him framed in the living-room door.

Sarika glared at him. Anger was her only defence against the hurt and humiliation she had suffered, and his overbearing, autocratic manner did nothing at that moment to ease the situation.

'You may own this house and fifty-one per cent of the Apex Company, but that doesn't mean that you own *me*, Sean O'Connor!' she hissed at him furiously.

'Sarika——'

'Don't you dare touch me!' she snapped when he took a pace towards her and raised his hand as if to grip her shoulder.

'Don't be an idiot, Sarika,' he frowned, dropping his hand to his side. 'I can understand that you're upset and even a little angry, but don't you realise that both Ayah and I have been nearly out of our minds worrying about you?'

'I'm old enough to take care of myself, thank you.'

'Dammit, woman, I'll make you see sense if it's the

last thing I do on this earth!' he barked at her, whipping her into the living-room and closing the door before she had time to guess his intentions.

'I said don't touch me!' she shouted at him, trying to wrench her arm from the grip of those steely fingers, and sheer desperation to get away from him made her react like a wild animal.

Her fingernails raked his cheek, and she was released at once to stare in horror at the raised weals against his tanned skin. Oh, God, what had she done? she wondered frantically when his hand went up to his cheek and came away with tiny drops of blood on his fingers. She wanted to apologise, but the fury in the eyes that blazed down into hers trapped the words in her throat.

'You little vixen, you're going to pay for this!' he muttered through his teeth, and pay for it she did.

She was clamped against his big, hard body with her arms trapped helplessly at her sides, and his mouth swooped down on to hers with a brutal force that crushed her lips against her teeth. She tried to cry out in protest, but her head was forced back with the pressure of his mouth until it felt as if her neck would snap, and she could neither move, nor make a sound while he continued the savage punishment. The physical pain was nothing compared to the pain which began to stir in the hidden depths of her soul. It confused and bewildered her, but from somewhere came the knowledge that this was not what she wanted from this man.

Sarika was released at last with a suddenness that made her stagger and clutch at the back of a chair to steady herself. She felt as if she had taken a mental and physical battering, and resentment kindled her anger once again into a blazing fury.

'I hate you, Sean O'Connor!' she hissed up at him. 'And I shall hate you until the day I die!'

She fled from the living-room, slamming the door behind her, and did not stop until she reached the safety of her bedroom, where she stood panting with angry tears in her eyes. *'Damn!'* she muttered to herself as she dabbed at her eyes with her fingers. In the scuffle with Sean she had dropped her handbag in the living-room, and nothing on earth would make her return there now to fetch it.

Her lips felt bruised, and they were visibly swollen when she caught a glimpse of herself in the dressing-table mirror. She turned away, and a distasteful thought occurred to her when she glanced about the room. If Ayah and her parents had gone to the trouble of redecorating her room *after* Sean had bought the house, then who had paid for it? Sean? Dear God, was there no end to this torture?

A knock on her door sent a wave of panic flooding through her, but it was Ayah who walked into her room a moment later.

'You left your handbag downstairs and Sean asked me to bring it to you.' A quizzical expression mingled with concern in her eyes as the bag exchanged hands. 'Sarika, *pyaari*, we have been so worried about you.'

'I'm sorry I rushed out and left you behind, but I've decided that I can't stay here,' Sarika informed the older woman. 'I'll get myself a flat somewhere, and I want you to come with me.'

'I can't do that,' stated Ayah firmly. 'I trained most of the staff in this house, and they work well under my supervision. I also promised that I would serve Sean as loyally as I served your parents in the past.'

Sarika stared at Ayah incredulously, then she was struck by yet another shattering discovery. 'You knew that this house belonged to Sean?'

'I knew,' Ayah admitted readily.

'Why didn't you tell me, Ayah?' Sarika cried out in anguish. 'Why?'

'Sean swore me to secrecy,' Ayah explained quietly, her eyes apologetic. 'He was afraid you would feel discomforted by the knowledge that he had bought the house, and he felt it would be easier for you to accept it once your parents were here with you, but things did not quite work out that way.'

'My God!' exclaimed Sarika sarcastically. 'The man is so thoughtful and considerate it makes me sick!'

'Sean is a wonderful man, *pyaari*,' Ayah rubbed salt into the wound. 'He was good to your parents, and he has been good to me.'

In Sarika's unhappy state of mind it seemed as if Ayah had turned traitor and, to make matters worse, a part of Sarika agreed with everything Ayah had said about Sean. He *was* a good man, and he was, in her own words, thoughtful and considerate, but knowing this filled Sarika with resentment, and made her all the more determined to go ahead with her plans.

'I've got to get away from here and find a place of my own.'

'In England that may be the accepted thing, Sarika, but this is India, and I will not allow you to go and live somewhere on your own.' Ayah's expression softened, and the liquid warmth of her dark eyes washed over Sarika. 'You are also the daughter I never had, and what mother would allow her daughter to go out and live on her own where she cannot care for her?'

Sarika could not argue against that. She did not want to go and leave Ayah behind, but to stay was going to take a great deal of courage, and she was not so sure that she would be able to cope.

Ayah left the room, and Sarika bathed and changed into something a little more colourful than the grey suit. She did not look forward to going down to dinner and having to face Sean, but she would have to take each embarrassing hurdle as it came, or brand herself a coward.

The atmosphere around the dinner table that evening was frozen. Ayah tried to encourage conversation, but she relinquished the effort in the end and concentrated on her food. Sarika could not eat. The red scars on Sean's cheek were a reminder of her humiliating loss of control, and the tenderness of her lips was an equally humiliating reminder of the painful punishment he had dished out. How had he explained those scratch marks to Ayah? she wondered frantically. She felt his eyes resting on her from time to time, but she did not dare look at him for fear of what she might see. Would it be anger, or mockery, or both? Sarika did not attempt to find out. She pushed the food around on her plate a while longer, settled for a cup of coffee, and finally excused herself to go up to her room.

She did not sleep very well that night; her mind was in a turmoil as it replayed everything that had happened since her return to Bombay, and it had all the proportions of a nightmare. Her decision to leave this house had been thwarted, and she was left with resentment and logic fighting a desperate battle for supremacy. Her mind had never before been in such a chaotic mess, and in order to bring about a certain amount of order she asked herself a few deeply probing questions. Did she resent the fact that Sean had taken charge of the Apex Company with the majority of shares? No! Did she resent the fact that he had bought the house from her father when her father had, in fact, considered selling it to help him out of his financial difficulties? Not really, she decided after a great deal of soul-searching. She could not blame anyone but herself for her humiliation, but it was nevertheless an uncomfortable feeling knowing that her home now belonged to Sean, and that, thanks to his kindness, she was allowed to stay on. Did she hate him? The answer to that question was negative, but she did not dare delve too deeply into the reason for it.

She awoke the following morning with a pounding headache which would not subside until she had swallowed down a couple of aspirins. How, she wondered desperately, was she going to get through the entire day without bumping into Sean?

Jaishree's telephone call after breakfast could not have come at a better time. She invited Sarika to accompany her to the home of friends for the day, and Sarika jumped at the opportunity to get out of the house and away from the man whose presence she was beginning to feel in every room.

'I'll pick you up in half an hour,' warned Jaishree, and Sarika did not keep her waiting. She was standing on the front steps when Jaishree's blue MG sped up the drive.

It was quite a journey down to Poona, which had long since been established as a major educational centre in India, but Sarika and Jaishree had a lot of news to catch up on.

'Tell me about the man you're going to marry,' Sarika prompted her friend after they had skirted over the subject of her parents' death. 'What is he like?'

'He is wonderful!' Jaishree sighed with a dreamy look in her eyes when she glanced briefly at Sarika. 'He works for a textile company, and we met five months ago at a party. Since then we have been seeing each other regularly, and we are going to be married in two weeks' time. It's going to be the longest two weeks in my life because, as you know, we are not allowed to see each other from the time the invitations go out until the day of our marriage.'

'Are your parents happy about it?'

'They weren't at first,' Jaishree confessed with a grimace, 'but they met Vinod's parents last weekend, and I think they are at last convinced that I made the right choice.'

'Am I going to be invited to the wedding?'

'Of course!' came the almost indignant reply. 'Your invitation will be delivered within the next few days, and so will Ayah's. We have also decided to invite that nice Mr O'Connor.'

Sarika's eyes widened in startled surprise. 'You know him?'

'Oh, yes!' Jaishree smiled. 'Ayah brought him to our home one evening, and we were all most impressed. He is so easy to talk to, and he had so many interesting stories to tell about the different countries he has visited.'

'Easy to talk to?' snorted Sarika cynically. 'He's overbearing, autocratic, egotistical, arrogant and insufferable!'

'My goodness, what a long list of adjectives!' Jaishree laughed teasingly, and the quick glance she darted at Sarika was speculative. 'He has most certainly made quite an impression on you, and no man has succeeded in doing that before . . . not even Gary.'

Not even Gary. Gary now reminded her of a worm. He had wriggled his way into her life, and she had fallen like an idiot for his handsome features and suave manner. For the first time in her life she had trusted a man, and he had let her down. She would never trust a man again. Gary had hoped for financial gain like everyone else. Sean was . . . what? He most certainly did not need her money. There was no reason at all, in fact, why he should want to strike up a closer relationship with her.

Sarika felt extraordinarily shattered at the thought. Sean did not need her in any way. There was nothing she could give him that he did not have already, and more. He had all the ingredients of a man who could be trusted, and yet she shied away from placing too much trust in him. Why?

'You're afraid of being hurt again, and I can understand that,' Jaishree resumed the conversation as if she had read Sarika's thoughts. 'You are shutting men out of your life by enlarging their faults to the extent that you are obliterating their good points, but you can't spend the rest of your life doing that, Sarika.'

'Giving your heart to someone and trusting them is like placing a whip in their hands, and I consider I've been hurt enough.'

'And you have allowed yourself to become cynical because of it.'

'Perhaps I have,' Sarika agreed thoughtfully. 'Perhaps I've simply become more cautious.'

'Caution is not always the parent of safety, if you will forgive me misquoting that old proverb,' argued Jaishree. 'Too much caution, where the heart is concerned, could make you lonely and embittered, and I would hate that to happen to you, my friend.'

Sarika smiled cynically, but during the ensuing silence she found her thoughts lingering on Jaishree's warning. Lonely and embittered! She knew what it was to be lonely, and perhaps she had already become embittered. She did not need anyone other than Ayah, but there was always that intense loneliness deep down inside her which she found so difficult to cope with, and it was increasing instead of dwindling.

You are afraid of being hurt again, and you are shutting men out of your life by enlarging their faults. Was that what she was doing?

Sean's rugged features leapt into her mind, and his dark eyes challenged her. A spark had ignited between them at their very first meeting, and Sarika would be lying to herself if she denied that she was dangerously attracted to him. He had made it clear from the start that he considered her a spoiled little girl, and yet, to prevent her discomfiture, he had withheld from her certain vital information concerning his true status. While she had been incapacitated with shock and grief, Sean had made the necessary arrangements for her parents' funeral, and she realised now that she had never thanked him. When she had needed support, he had given it without waiting for her to ask, and it was on his shoulder that she had shed the most tears. When, for the first time yesterday, he had shown visible concern for her safety, she had repaid him by raking his face like a wildcat, and thinking about it now made her cringe inwardly with shame.

That nice Mr O'Connor, Jaishree had called him. *Nice* was not exactly the adjective Sarika would have chosen for him. *Interesting* was a more applicable word. Interesting, vital, and very male. She did not need to be told what he thought of her. He considered her beautiful, but spoiled and too accustomed to having her own way. She was certain that, if her name had to appear on a list of possibilities, he would cross it off without a second thought.

That hurt—that really hurt! She did not want to be crossed off, overlooked, ignored. She wanted . . . Sarika pulled her thoughts up sharply. She had to stop thinking of Sean in this way. He was a man; a member of the sex she had sworn never to trust again, and she had to go on remembering that if she did not want to find herself falling in love all over again with someone who could never care for her in return.

The home of Stephen and Claudia Nicholson, Jaishree's friends, was situated on the outskirts of Poona in a quiet suburb. They were a bright, cheerful, and amusing couple, and Sarika actually found herself shaking off her depression and deep sorrow. Accompanying Jaishree on this visit provided exactly the right antidote Sarika had needed, and the Nicholsons' son, Michael, provided further entertainment by taking Sarika and Jaishree to the stables after lunch to show them the chestnut foal which had been born only a few days prior to their visit. It was still wobbly on its legs, and very wary of the attention it was receiving.

Sarika was also not unaware of the attention *she* was receiving from Michael, a lanky, fair-haired young man a few years her senior. She was conscious of his grey eyes watching every move she made, and she had also witnessed that flicker of something more than interest in his glances. She had encountered this sort of thing often enough not to let it trouble her, but her aloofness seemed to intrigue him rather than repulse him.

The day had passed so swiftly that it was with some regret that Sarika said goodbye to the Nicholsons, but Michael was determined not to end their acquaintance there.

'Will you have dinner with me one evening when I'm in Bombay?' he asked when he and his parents accompanied Sarika and Jaishree out to the MG parked in their drive.

Sarika had her usual refusal ready, but she hesitated. Perhaps it would not be such a bad idea to see Michael occasionally if it would help take her mind off the dangerous feelings Sean was arousing in her.

'I can't promise anything,' she said with some caution, 'but please do give me a call when you're in Bombay.'

She got into the car beside Jaishree and, with a final wave, the MG sped down the drive and out through the gates.

'Am I wrong in thinking Michael made a date with you?' Jaishree questioned Sarika as they sped away from the house.

'He asked me to have dinner with him one evening when he happened to be in Bombay.'

Jaishree cast a quick glance in Sarika's direction. 'What did you think of him?'

'He's . . . nice,' Sarika said for want of a better word.

'He couldn't take his eyes off you all day,' Jaishree winked impishly at Sarika.

'So I noticed,' murmured Sarika dryly, then she directed the conversation elsewhere. 'I thought Stephen and Claudia were two of the loveliest people I've met in a long time.'

'They used to live in Bombay before they moved to Poona, and they have been friends of my family for many years,' Jaishree enlightened her. 'Michael has always been like a brother to me, and I would like to see him married one day to a nice young woman.'

Sarika glanced suspiciously at her friend. 'A young woman like myself, perhaps?'

'Perhaps,' Jaishree smiled a little slyly, and Sarika was instantly annoyed.

'Jaishree, if you planned this trip today with the intention of indulging in a bout of matchmaking, then you can——'

'Wait!' her friend interrupted her sharply. 'I planned

this outing today for the simple reason that I felt you needed a break away from home after your terrible ordeal this past week. I had no idea that Michael would be at home today, and if I appear to be indulging in a bout of matchmaking, as you put it, then it is because of the way he looked at you, and for no other reason. I also happened to be teasing you.'

Sarika's annoyance turned to guilt. She was not usually in the habit of jumping to conclusions, and she had never before objected to being teased. Sarika knew that Jaishree had meant no harm, but everything inside her had suddenly come into revolt when she had suspected her friend of wanting to pair her off with Michael. Too much had happened to unnerve her since her return to Bombay. Her parents were dead, she had to come to a decision about her future, but ... *dammit*, there had been no need to take it out on her friend.

'I'm sorry,' she apologised. 'I guess I'm just a little touchy.'

'That's understandable,' Jaishree accepted her explanation readily, and the rest of the journey back to Bombay was taken up with Jaishree discussing her wedding arrangements.

Sarika did not listen to everything her friend was telling her. Her mind was too occupied with her own pressing thoughts. She needed to be occupied; she needed to work, and if she was to stay on in the house with Sean, then she would have to earn the right to do so. She had sat around idle long enough and, as the only other shareholder in the Apex Company, she was going to do exactly what her father had intended her to do when he had sent her away to university.

Sean was not at home when Jaishree dropped her off at the house. He was dining out with friends, Ayah informed her, and he was not expected back until late that evening. Sarika was disappointed. She had wanted to discuss her plans with him, but now it would have to wait until the following day.

She went down to breakfast early the Sunday morning, but once again her discussion with Sean had to be postponed. He had gone out for the day, and Ayah had no idea when to expect him back.

Patience was not one of Sarika's virtues that particular day. She filled the hours swimming and sunbathing, and yet the day dragged infuriatingly. Ayah and Sarika sat down to dinner that evening without Sean, and by ten o'clock Sarika had given up hope of confronting him with her decision. Frustrated, she went up to her room to take a bath before going to bed, and she was pulling back the covers to get between the sheets when the stillness of the night was disturbed by the sound of the Land Rover coming up the drive.

She hesitated for barely a second before she pushed her feet into soft mules. She slid her arms into the wide sleeves of her silk robe, and was still tying the belt about her waist when she left her room and hurried down the stairs into the hall. The front door opened, and Sean stepped into the hall at the same time as Sarika. In white tennis shorts and shirt, with a racquet in one hand and a white sweater slung across his shoulder, he presented an awe-inspiring image of masculine fitness, and Sarika stood there staring at him as if she had never seen him before in her life. His muscled thighs and calves were tanned as deeply as his face and arms, and the sheer height and breadth of him when he closed the door and walked towards her was enough to make her heart race madly.

'Well, well, well!' His eyebrows rose in sardonic amusement as he looked her up and down, and she suspected that he had had a little too much to drink. 'I never thought I'd ever come home to find you waiting up for me, Sarika.'

She swallowed nervously and wondered if she ought not to leave it until the morning, but then she squared her shoulders and followed him into the living-room. 'I want to talk to you.'

'Do you?' he smiled mockingly, flinging his racquet

and sweater on to a chair. 'Or is this what you were hoping for?'

She was pulled into his arms and his mouth came down on hers with a precision that caught her off her guard. She felt insulted, but for long dizzying seconds she was too stunned to react.

CHAPTER SIX

THE world began to right itself when Sarika felt Sean's hands roaming over her body in an intimate exploration that seemed to burn her through the silk of her robe. Her mind rejected the sensations he seemed to arouse with such ease, but her treacherous body responded to the sensual demand of his lips and hands. Logic fought a lone battle against the alien desires that swept through her, but it was the realisation that this meant nothing to him that finally made her go rigid and cold in his arms.

She somehow managed to get her hands in between them and, with an unexpected burst of strength, she pushed him away from her. She was shaking so much that she could scarcely stand unsupported as she faced him with a blaze of fury in her tawny eyes. 'If you do that to me again, Sean O'Connor, so help me I'll——'

'You'll what?' he prompted derisively when she choked back the rest of her words. 'Dig your nails into the other side of my face?'

She stared up at the faint scars her nails had left on his cheek and clenched her hands at her sides until her nails bit into her soft palms. 'If you continue to misunderstand me, then I might just do that!'

'Okay, you little vixen, so you waited up to talk to me and not for the pleasure of my kisses,' he mocked her as he turned away to pour himself a whisky. 'I feel slighted, but I guess I'll overcome it.'

Sarika bit down hard on her trembling lip while she fought to regain her composure, and she waited until he turned again to face her. 'I'm coming to the office as from tomorrow morning.'

The ice tinkled in his glass, jarring her nerves as he raised it to his lips and swallowed down a mouthful. 'I'm afraid I can't allow that.'

'Since I'm part owner of Apex I don't think you can stop me.'

The silence was rife with antagonism as they stood glaring at each other, then he lessened the distance between them in a few long, angry strides. 'You expect to walk in and take over your father's position,' he snapped his fingers, 'just like that?'

'I'm not quite the idiot you think I am, Sean,' she protested, refusing to be intimidated by his menacing attitude as he towered over her. 'I know I can't step into my father's position without the necessary experience, so I intend to work my way up to it, starting from the drawing office.'

'There aren't any vacancies in the drawing office.'

'There doesn't have to be,' she argued, raising her chin to meet his angry glance. 'I'll find something to do, and a place to do it in.'

Angry defiance brought a sparkle to her eyes and a glow to her cheeks which enhanced her beauty, and Sean's eyes narrowed speculatively as he studied her intently. 'You're determined, aren't you.'

'And you're equally determined to stop me,' she retaliated cynically. 'I wonder why?'

Sean was silent for a moment, then he laughed unexpectedly, but it was a harsh, mocking laugh that raked unpleasantly across her nerve ends. 'I can imagine the sinister thoughts running wild at this moment through that pretty little head of yours.'

'Can you blame me?' she challenged him.

'Not entirely,' he shook his head, 'but you're way off the mark, honey, and that's a fact.'

'Explain to me, then, why you don't want me in the office?'

His expression was suddenly strangely hooded. 'You've had a rough time, and you need a break before you get yourself involved with the company.'

Everyone was so concerned about giving her a break that it was beginning to sicken her. 'I can't sit around doing nothing, and I want to earn the right to those shares.'

Sean swallowed down the remainder of his whisky and put down his glass before he slumped into a chair with his legs stretched out comfortably in front of him. His eyes were still narrowed, but his mouth twisted in a derisive smile as he sat there looking up at her slim, straight figure. 'What really bugs you is having to live in a house that now belongs to me.'

He was shrewd and clever, but she was not going to be persuaded to change her mind. 'I'm not going to deny that having to live here is part of the reason why I need to get out and work,' she confessed.

'This is your home, Sarika, for as long as you want to stay,' he reminded her with that calmness which always seemed to infuriate her. 'That was the understanding I had with your parents, and the same applies to you.'

'I don't want your charity!' she retorted distastefully.

'I'm being sensible, not charitable,' he pointed out tolerantly. 'Pretty soon now this house is simply going to be a place which I could call home when I'm in Bombay, so why shouldn't you stay on here with Ayah?'

Sarika felt something cold clutch at her heart. 'What do you mean?'

'I mean, Sarika, that I travel a lot,' he explained in the same tone of voice one would use to a child. 'My home base is in the United States, but I have corporate companies in several other countries, and Apex is now one of them.'

'You mean Apex has become a part of—of——'

'Premier International,' he filled in for her when she faltered incredulously. 'My father started the company twenty years ago, and it now consists of smaller companies which can cope with building and engineering requirements in many parts of the world.'

She had heard of Premier International, and she knew the vastness of this particular organisation, but instead of being impressed she was aroused to an unreasonable anger. 'I'm surprised you didn't buy my father out completely while you were about it!'

'It always pays to leave the original owner with a substantial part of the shares,' Sean smiled mockingly as he lit a cheroot and blew the smoke towards the ceiling. 'That way I know that my interests will be well taken care of.'

'I thought you said that my father had intentions of retiring from the business,' she retorted suspiciously.

'That's what he said,' Sean acknowledged, 'but I had hoped that I would have time to make him change his mind, and I think I would have succeeded.'

'All the more reason then why I should learn the business as soon as I can,' she took advantage of his remark.

'Unless, of course, you want to sell out to an interested party.'

Sarika's back stiffened with resentment and indignation. 'Do you think me incapable of doing my father's job?'

'It was merely a suggestion,' shrugged Sean, drawing hard on his cheroot as he studied her speculatively through the cloud of smoke he exhaled. 'There aren't many women who could fill a position like that.'

'So that's it!' she exploded furiously. 'It's sex discrimination! Because I'm a woman you would much rather I sell out my shares than take an active interest in the business. Well, I'm not going to do that, Sean O'Connor! I'm a woman, yes, but I'm also a qualified architect, and there's no reason why I should have to step aside for any man. I'll be at the office as from tomorrow, I'll learn all there is to know, and before long I'll show you just what this *woman* can do!'

'That was quite a speech, honey, but speeches are not what I shall expect from you if you're determined to come to the office tomorrow.' There was a hint of contempt in the dark eyes that raked her from head to foot. 'I'm going to be mean. I'm going to give you two weeks before I throw you in at the deep end, and you'd better know how to swim.'

He picked up his things and strode out of the living-room, leaving Sarika to stare after him with wide eyes that were beginning to reflect a hint of uncertainty. Had she not perhaps bitten off a little more than she could chew this time? He was going to give her two weeks. What could she accomplish in such a short space of time? There was no sense in thinking that he had not meant what he had said. He would give her two weeks before he threw her in at the deep end, and, as he had warned, she had better know how to swim.

Talking about something theroetically and actually putting it into practice were two different things, Sarika discovered after her first few days at the office. There were so many facets to the Apex company that her mind boggled, and learning to take over her father's job was a mammoth task she would not have been forced to accomplish in two weeks if she had not goaded Sean into issuing that challenge. Sean was not going to help her, she had known that from the start, but she also knew that he was aware of every move she made, and she could almost see him observing her with a patronising smile while she worked at a frantic pace all day until she fell into bed exhausted at night.

Sarika did not venture into the administrative side at once, and she concentrated first of all on the working procedures. She had a good memory, and a mind that absorbed facts, so it was not until her fourth day that she took that giant leap into her father's office. Sarika accompanied Sean to the office as usual the Thursday morning, and they did not speak as they entered the building and walked across the mirrored foyer with its exotic potted plants. The girl behind the reception desk could not take her eyes off Sean when they walked towards the lift, but Sean barely noticed her. He thumbed the button, the doors slid open, and they stepped into the steel cage.

'What floor this morning?' Sean broke the stony silence between them with his mocking query, but Sarika was determined not to let him unnerve her.

'Fifth,' she answered abruptly, and his eyebrows rose in sardonic amusement as he pressed the required button.

'You're going for the jackpot this morning, are you?'

'I have to go for it some time, don't I?' she smiled up at him coldly. 'You set that ridiculous time limit, so don't blame me if I appear to be speeding things up a little.'

'You've been burning the candle at both ends these past few days, and in this game you could burn yourself out if you're not careful.'

'I must remind you again that you were the one who set the time limit,' she said, a glacial look in her tawny eyes when they met his.

A deep frown settled between his dark brows. 'I didn't intend you to wear yourself out in the process.'

'What did you imagine I'd do?' she demanded in an icy, controlled voice. 'Did you think I'd run like a frightened rabbit at the prospect of learning to take over my father's position in this company?'

His narrowed gaze slid over her, from her hair which was coiled into a neat chignon in the nape of her neck, down to her comfortable shoes. He made her feel as if she had been weighed and found wanting, and that was not a feeling she could cope with very well at that moment.

'I don't know what I expected,' he said as they stepped out of the lift on the fifth floor, 'but it's obvious I can't credit you with being a coward.'

He walked away from her towards his office at the end of the passage, and left her standing there with the feeling that she had been accused of something rather than complimented. She was baffled as she followed him down the passage, but she shrugged it off the moment she entered her father's book-lined office with its enormous mahogany desk.

Memories came flooding back of the last time she had seen her father alive. That had been eight months ago, and she could still see him sitting there behind his desk with his favourite cigar between his fingers.

'You will complete your studies, and you will forget about this idea of yours to open up a boutique. Do I make myself clear?' he had shouted at her, and she had turned away from him without saying a word. She had walked out of his office, and had not seen him again before her return to England.

The memory hurt. It could have been so different, but fate had decided, and Sarika could not put back the clock no matter how much she wished she could do so. This was *now*, and she had to make the best of the situation.

She trailed her fingers lightly over the polished surface of the desk and sat down gingerly in the high-backed swivel chair. It felt odd sitting there behind her father's desk. She could almost see him standing next to her, puffing his cigar and looking smug.

'Well, here I am, Dad,' she spoke her thoughts aloud. 'Right where you always wanted me.'

'Your father always used to talk to himself.' Sarika looked up sharply to see Miranda Davis smiling at her from across the room. 'It's good to have you in the office, Sarika, and please don't hesitate to buzz me if you need any help.'

She gestured towards the intercom system on the desk as she spoke, and walked out of the office, her sensible shoes making no sound on the carpeted floor.

Sarika swallowed nervously. She was certainly going to need assistance, and Miranda Davis was perhaps the right person to give it to her. Miranda was a woman of almost forty, and she had been Dave Maynesfield's secretary for many years. She knew every aspect of the administrative side as well as Sarika's father had done, and now, Sarika imagined, she was most probably also acting as Sean's secretary.

A little sigh escaped her as she put aside her handbag. She had to acquaint herself with her new environment, and, opening one of the top-drawers in the desk, she studied its contents. Her glance fell at once on a gold pen she had given her father some years ago as a birthday present. It was still in its box and it had presumably never been used. Her mouth tightened and, slamming the drawer shut, she worked her way systematically through the contents of the other drawers.

Sarika had never had difficulty in grasping something, but she had never considered it a blessing until now. She was determined to succeed at what she was doing and, with Miranda's help, she found herself settling slowly into her father's position at the office. The weekend came too soon, and with it came that stab of anxiety. She had one more week to prove herself, and she had a feeling that Sean was not going to be lenient.

The weekend started on a sour note when Ayah came up to Sarika's room after dinner that Friday evening. 'You are treating Sean badly. You speak to him only when he speaks to you, and you are creating an atmosphere in this house which is unpleasant and unnecessary.'

Ayah's accusation came so unexpectedly that it took several seconds for Sarika to formulate a reply. 'If there is an atmosphere, then I apologise, but you can't say that I haven't been civil.'

'Civil?' Ayah threw up her hands and the gold bangles tinkled against her wrist. 'Do you call it civil to snap your answers at him when he has asked you a question? Sarika, the man has been trying very hard to make you feel at home, and I am ashamed of the way you repay him. When you were a child I taught you manners, but it seems I shall have to start over again!'

She walked out of the room, her white sari floating about her, and Sarika stood there speechless as the door closed behind the older woman's ample figure. She wished she could explain to Ayah how she felt, but she could not even explain to herself the reason for this unfamiliar turbulence in her usually placid nature. Every time Sean came near her she could feel her hackles rising, and she would invariably prepare herself for battle. It was as if she had acquired a built-in defence mechanism which kicked over every time she saw him, but she was not quite sure what she was defending herself against.

Sean left the house early the Saturday morning; Sarika saw him from her bedroom window, and only then did she go down to breakfast. Ayah shook her head as if she suspected the reason for Sarika's lateness in coming down to breakfast, but this time she did not say anything. Sarika wished Sean would stay away all day, but he returned just before lunch and poured himself a whisky which he drank out on the terrace until Ayah called them into the dining-room.

'What about a game of tennis?' Sean suggested when they finally left the luncheon table and went upstairs.

'I would rather go for a swim, thank you,' Sarika declined in a cool voice as she turned away from him to enter her bedroom, and she closed the door firmly behind her as if something had warned her that he might follow her inside.

She realised that her heart was beating against her ribs as if she had been running. *You're scared*, a little voice accused. Scared of what? she wondered. *Scared of yourself and your own feelings*, came the answer, but Sarika brushed it aside cynically and changed into her bikini.

It was a hot, humid afternoon, and she had settled herself comfortably on the recliner beside the pool when Sean appeared beside her in blue swimming trunks and a towel draped across one tanned shoulder. His long muscular legs were covered with short dark hair, and the aura of raw masculinity that surrounded him was so overpowering that her body went oddly limp and heavy on the recliner while she lay there looking up at him.

'You don't mind if I join you, do you?' he broke the silence between them, the silver medallion about his throat glinting in the sun, and Sarika pulled herself together with an effort when she saw his dark glance flicking over her scantily clad body.

'It's your pool,' she replied stiffly, sitting up with a jerk.

'I'm master of this house, and I can do as I please, is that what you're saying?' he demanded in a lazy drawl.

'Exactly!' she snapped.

Sean's mouth tightened as he flung his towel on to a chair and studied her with his hands resting on his lean hips. 'You're looking for trouble, Sarika, and you're going to get it if you're not careful.'

'Are you threatening me, by any chance?'

'I'm not threatening you,' he corrected, a dangerous flicker in his eyes. 'I'm warning you.'

'Thanks!' she snapped again as she got to her feet.

'Where the hell do you think you're going?' he demanded harshly.

'I'm going up to my room,' she glared at him as she walked to where she had left her towel and her robe. 'Any objections?'

'You came out for a swim, and that's what you're going to do!' he insisted with a menacing look on his face.

He moved with the speed of lightning, and before she had time to guess his intentions she was being lifted high in his arms. She knew then what he intended doing, but it was too late. One moment she could still feel the hard, bunched-up muscles of his arms about her, and the next she was flying through the air. There was just enough time to draw breath before she hit the water, and her body went down like a rock to the bottom at the deep end of the pool before she could right herself and kick herself up to the surface.

'You despicable beast!' she cried chokingly, wiping the lank, wet hair away from her eyes, but her heart almost stopped beating when she saw Sean diving into the water.

She turned and tried to get to the edge of the pool before he reached her, but trying to get away from him in that environment was like trying to escape from someone in a nightmare. Her limbs felt heavy, and her movements retarded. Fear almost choked her, and she had difficulty in suppressing the scream that rose in her throat when a heavy hand gripped her shoulder and pulled her away from the tiled edge.

'You're not going anywhere just yet, Sarika,' he smiled at her in a devilish way that made her all the more determined to escape.

'Get away from me!' she cried, making a renewed attempt to escape his strong hands, but her efforts were futile.

His arm was hard about her waist, and her body was clamped against his in a way that she could feel the roughness of his thighs brushing against hers while he trod water. Being so close to him, flesh against flesh, was in itself an intimacy that set her pulses racing madly, and she clutched helplessly at his broad, damp shoulders as the cloudless sky dipped and swayed crazily.

'I did warn you that you were looking for trouble, didn't I?' he mocked her, his strong teeth white against his skin as he eased her towards the side of the pool where he could detain her with more ease.

'You had no right to throw me into the pool!' she accused, her fingers touching the smooth tiles, and she breathed a little easier when he released her.

'Be thankful I didn't pull you over my knee and spank you.'

'You wouldn't have dared!'

'Is that a challenge?'

He gripped the edge of the pool and moved towards her with a dangerous glitter in his eyes. His dark hair was plastered to his forehead, and the drops of water glistening on his tanned, rugged face added a devastatingly attractive touch to his appearance. She knew the danger of challenging him, and she turned from him to rest her arms along the tiled edge of the kidney-shaped pool.

'Oh, go away!' she groaned, resting her forehead

against her arms, and wishing suddenly she had not been so foolish as to pit her wits against him.

'Stop fighting me, honey.' His arm circled her waist from behind, and when his hand came to rest against her flat stomach she went hot despite the coolness of the water. 'I'm not your enemy, and there's no reason for you to consider me a threat in any way.'

If only he knew! His nearness and his touch against her bare flesh was threatening her at that very moment. She could feel herself weakening and becoming suffused with a longing she did not dare analyse.

'Please let me go,' she begged, her voice horribly unsteady while she still fought desperately for control.

He removed his arm from about her waist, but he stayed close to her in the water. 'If we have to work together as partners, then we could at least be civil to each other.'

'Partners?' she snorted disparagingly, turning her head to risk a glance at him. 'I'm simply a small cog in that big wheel which comprises your entire organisation. Although I possess shares in Apex, I'm no more really than an employee of yours, so we could never actually call ourselves *partners*.'

'You're forgetting something,' he mocked her. 'As the only other shareholder in Apex you're automatically elected on to the board of directors at Premier International, and that makes us partners whether you like it or not.'

It was an overwhelming discovery, and she was totally unprepared for it. Her head went down on to her arms again, and she groaned, 'Oh, God!'

'What's the problem now?' Sean demanded with a hint of exasperation in his deep, gravelly voice.

'I've only just realised that doing my father's job entails a hell of a lot more than I'd originally imagined.'

'Do you want to throw in the towel?'

'Never!' she cried adamantly, raising her head to meet his glance squarely. 'I don't give up that easily!'

'I didn't think you would.' He smiled at her in a way

that made her feel as if her bones were melting, then his expression altered, and his eyes were thoughtfully intent upon her face. 'You're quite a woman, Sarika, and I must admit that my opinion of you is changing rapidly.'

'For the better, I hope?' she asked before she could stop herself, and his smile deepened with mockery as his fingers tapped her lightly against the cheek in chastisement.

'Now you're fishing for compliments.'

'Heaven forbid!' she laughed away her embarrassment and the feelings he was arousing when his punishing touch became a caress, and he did not try to stop her this time when she lifted herself out of the pool and walked to where she had left her towel and her robe.

CHAPTER SEVEN

SARIKA was seated at her father's desk studying the plans for a housing scheme which was to be built by a consortium on the outskirts of the city of Agra, which lay some six hundred miles north of Bombay. She was frowning down at the plans when Sean walked into the office.

'Aren't you going out to lunch?' he asked, and Sarika glanced at her watch to see that it was after one, but keeping to a rigid time schedule was something she had ignored during her second week at Apex.

'Have these plans been approved?' she questioned him without answering his query.

'Not yet,' Sean informed her when he stood beside her chair and studied the plans over her shoulder. 'They were drawn up to the requirements of the consortium, and we'll be meeting with their representative before the final plans are drawn up. Why do you ask?'

'I see no reason for the houses to be bunched up together when there's sufficient space to allow for recreational areas. The people who are going to be living in these houses will have children, and if one pushed the houses farther out on the east and west side, then one could erect a park here,' she jabbed a slim finger at the plan, 'and there.'

'That's not a bad idea,' Sean agreed. 'I have to fly up to Agra tomorrow morning, so I suggest you make arrangements to meet with the consortium's representative, then we could fly up there together.'

Sarika's heart lurched nervously. 'You want me to handle it?'

'Why not?' he asked, his eyes narrowed and intent upon her face as he seated himself on the corner of her desk and crossed his arms over his wide chest.

'You're throwing me into the deep end a little too early, aren't you?' she questioned him mockingly.

'This is shallow water, honey,' he assured her. 'The contract is ours whether they approve your new ideas or not, so there's nothing to lose, and plenty to gain.'

Sarika swallowed convulsively. If this was the shallow end, then she dreaded to think what it would be like at the deep end. She rolled up the plans and pushed them aside to search for her handbag. 'I think I'll go out to lunch after all.'

The humidity hit her like a damp sheet when they stepped out of the air-conditioned foyer into the sunlight, and she could almost feel the perspiration breaking out all over her body.

'I'm having lunch with a client, so don't expect me back before three,' Sean warned as they parted company.

Since the weekend their relationship had been less chilly, and Sarika had to admit that she preferred the situation as it was at that moment. They were polite to each other, even friendly, but nothing more.

When she returned to the office an hour later she put a call through to Agra and, when Sean finally returned, she could tell him that she had made the necessary arrangements to accompany him the following day.

'Have you ever been to the Taj Mahal in Agra?' she asked out of curiosity before she left his office to return to her own.

'No, I haven't.'

'If there's time it would be worth taking a drive out to it.'

Sean leaned back in his chair to study her through narrowed eyes, then he smiled briefly. 'If there's time I think I would like that.'

Sarika felt a little embarrassed at the thought that her remark might have been misconstrued as an invitation. She turned quickly before he could see her colour rising, and went back to her own office, but everything else was temporarily forgotten when she studied the plans once again and made sketches of her own ideas which she hoped to put forward.

The telephone rang an hour later, and she reached out for the receiver without looking up from the plans. 'Yes?'

'There's a Michael Nicholson on the line for you,' Miranda Davis told her.

'Michael Nicholson?' Sarika repeated blankly, looking up suddenly to find her glance colliding with Sean's as he entered her office.

'He insists that he knows you personally,' Miranda elaborated, and quite suddenly Sarika remembered.

She had become so involved with learning her father's job since meeting the Nicholsons that she had almost forgotten the fair-haired Michael, and the blush that stained her cheeks was partly because of the mocking glint of Sean's eyes when he approached her desk and seated himself on the corner to watch her.

'Put him through,' she instructed Miranda with an abruptness which was brought on by nervousness, and the next moment Michael's voice came over the line.

'I know this is rather late in the day to call you, Sarika, but are you perhaps free this evening to have dinner with me?'

A polite refusal hovered on her lips, but the mockery in Sean's eyes made her change her mind. 'I'm free this evening.'

'I have your address,' said Michael. 'Would it be all right if I called for you at seven?'

'That would be perfect,' Sarika agreed.

'See you later, then.'

The line went dead, and Sarika replaced the receiver on its cradle feeling a little irritated with herself.

'Is Michael Nicholson an admirer?' came the mocking query.

'He's an acquaintance,' corrected Sarika, keeping her eyes lowered to the plans on her desk. 'Jaishree knows his family, and she took me out to Poona to meet them the weekend before last.'

'I gather you're having dinner with him this evening.'

'That's correct.' She controlled her features and risked a glance up at him. 'Any reason why I shouldn't?'

'No reason,' Sean shrugged carelessly, rising to his feet. 'Just as long as you remember that you have an important day ahead of you tomorrow.'

'I'll remember . . . *sir*,' she dared to mock him lightly, then her expression sobered. 'What did you want to see me about?'

'It was nothing important,' he said with a shuttered expression, then he strode out of her office and left her sitting there with the curious sensation that something vital had slipped from her grasp.

'I'm so glad you're dining out with Sean this evening,' said Ayah when Sarika telephoned to let her know about the arrangements she had made.

'I'm not dining out with Sean,' Sarika corrected her with a startled look on her face. 'I'm dining with Michael Nicholson.'

'But I thought——' Ayah broke off abruptly, obviously as confused as Sarika. 'Never mind,' she ended the conversation briskly.

Sarika sat for some time staring straight ahead of her with a puzzled frown creasing her smooth brow. Why, she wondered, had Ayah imagined she would be dining with Sean? She shrugged it off eventually with the thought that Sean must also be dining out, and that Ayah had naturally assumed that they would be dining together.

When she arrived home that evening she went straight up to her room to bath and change. She did not see Sean, and the only time she saw Ayah was when she went downstairs to wait for Michael. Sarika had a vague suspicion that Ayah was upset about something, but Michael arrived a short while later, and that left Sarika with no time to ponder the thought.

Dining out with Michael was rather pleasant and relaxing except for the fact that her mind was occupied with the meeting she had arranged for the following day. Michael was attentive all the same, and he made no effort to hide how he felt about her. She tried to warn him that she had no interest in a serious relationship with a man, but Michael was not dissuaded when she proffered a tentative friendship.

'We'll take it from there,' he said confidently and, at her request, he took her home early.

The living-room light was on when she entered the house, and she crossed the hall towards the door which stood slightly ajar. She pushed it open, and was surprised to see Sean sprawled in a chair with a glass of whisky in the one hand and a cheroot in the other. Dressed in jeans, white canvas shoes and a blue striped shirt, he did not look as if he had left the house that evening. What had happened to his dinner date? An uncomfortable thought leapt into her mind. Was it possible that he had wanted to invite her out to dinner, and that Michael had beaten him to it? It would explain Ayah's confusion on the telephone, and it would also explain why his visit to her office that afternoon had suddenly lost its importance.

'I trust you enjoyed your evening?' his derisive remark cut into her thoughts, and she stood there staring at him for several disquieting seconds before she spoke.

'Have you been waiting up for me?' she counter-questioned, trying not to look at his sun-browned chest where his shirt had been unbuttoned almost to the waist.

'I should imagine you're past the age where someone would wait up to make sure you arrive home safely,' he replied cuttingly, and Sarika had the extraordinary feeling that she was being chastised for something she had done.

'I understood from Ayah that you would be dining out this evening.'

The ice tinkled in his glass as he swallowed down a mouthful of whisky. 'It was cancelled.'

'Why?'

'Mind your own business!'

'Did the cancellation of your dinner appointment annoy you, or are you usually bad-tempered at this time of night?' she probed, ignoring his rudeness.

'Go to bed, Sarika!' he ordered harshly, swallowing down the last of his drink and getting up to pour himself another. 'We're leaving for the airport at seven-thirty in the morning, and I don't want to be kept waiting.'

Sarika hesitated. She was almost convinced now that he had intended taking her out to dinner, and she could not suppress a stab of disappointment. She considered confronting him with her suspicions, but something warned her not to prolong the conversation. He was quite obviously in a foul mood, and she had no desire to involve herself in a verbal battle with him at that late hour. She said good-night and went up to her room as he had instructed, but for some reason she did not go to sleep until she heard him walk past her door to his suite.

They left the house early the following morning in Sean's Land Rover. There was no sign of the mood he had laboured under the previous evening, but Sarika remained cautious during the long drive out to the airport. It was only when they got into the eight-seater aircraft belonging to Apex that the corners of her mouth lifted in an impish smile.

'Are you feeling better this morning?' she asked, slanting a glance at him when they were seated across the narrow aisle from each other.

He studied her for a moment, his rugged features expressionless, then he reached out a hand and slid his fingers beneath the heavy roll of hair which she had coiled into the nape of her neck. His touch seemed to burn her, then she was pulled roughly towards him, and she was kissed long and hard on the mouth before she was released.

'I feel much better now,' he smiled at her mockingly while his hands sought the seat-belt and fastened it about him.

Sarika was flushed and breathless while the pilot taxied the aircraft towards the runway, and her hands were trembling to the extent that it took her longer than usual to snap her seat-belt into position. No matter how much she tried she could not obliterate the feel of his hard mouth against hers, and his prolonged, mocking stare almost totally unnerved her. She glanced at Sean when the aircraft's engines began to rev in preparation for take-off, and quite suddenly the situation seemed so ridiculous that her clear laughter rang out above the noise of the engines.

'That was a mean thing to do,' she accused him as the aircraft sped along the runway and finally soared into the air.

'Yes, wasn't it,' Sean agreed, his smile deepening for a brief moment, then he opened his briefcase and took out a small pile of documents.

Sarika was ignored after that, and she could not decide whether she was relieved or annoyed. She was positive that it was unintentional, but he had certainly succeeded in arousing her interest these past weeks. She was intrigued as she had never been before, but she had to remember that soon he would be gone, and then he would be no more than a voice on the telephone, or a signature at the bottom of a business letter. It was a thought that hurt, and she refused to dwell on it for the moment.

Agra was a commercial and industrial city situated on the banks of the Jumna river, and Sarika pointed out the barley, wheat and cotton fields to Sean when they came in low to land. Sean had arranged for a car to be placed at their disposal, and he drove her from the airport into the city.

'I'll pick you up here at one,' he instructed when they arrived at the building which housed the offices of the consortium, and a mocking smile curved his mouth when she got out of the car. 'Good luck!'

He drove away and left Sarika standing there with the feeling that she was going to need all the luck she could get.

Clutching her briefcase in one hand and the plans in the other, she turned and entered the air-conditioned building with a feeling of trepidation. Mr Ramdhuni's office was on the second floor, and he was expecting her, the young Indian girl at reception told Sarika. The lift carried her soundlessly up to the required level, and a few minutes later she was shown into the office of a lean Indian gentleman with a hint of grey in the dark hair slicked back so severely from his broad forehead.

'Ah, Miss Maynesfield!' He rose to welcome her and, gesturing towards the tray on his desk, asked, 'Shall we have tea before we get down to business?'

'Thank you,' Sarika smiled. 'Tea would be most welcome.'

'I would like to offer my sympathies with the unfortunate demise of your parents,' he said when they sat drinking their tea. 'When I first discussed the plans for this housing scheme it was with your father, and it seems strange that I should now continue those discussions with his daughter.'

Sarika felt herself stiffen automatically in defence. 'Do you object to that, Mr Ramdhuni?'

'Not at all,' he assured her hastily, putting aside his empty cup. 'I shall be very interested to hear what suggestions you have to make.'

She drained her own cup of tea, and the pleasantries were over as they got down to business. She spread out the draft of the plans which had been drawn up to his specification, and produced her own rough draft of what she had in mind.

If Sarika had imagined that it would be easy convincing Mr Ramdhuni that his plans were impractical, then she was mistaken. He put up an argument which almost had her floored during the ensuing hours, and when she glanced up at the wall clock to see the hands shifting rapidly towards one o'clock, it was out of sheer desperation that she asked: 'Mr Ramdhuni, do you have children?'

'I have two sons and a daughter.'

He looked a little puzzled that their meeting had suddenly veered towards the personal, but Sarika could see that she had touched on a subject which afforded him a great deal of pride and pleasure.

'Do they have a place where they can play?' she shot the question at him.

'Oh, yes, there is a public park just around the corner from our home,' he replied at once, and her triumphant smile made him realise that he had walked neatly into the trap she had set for him. 'That was a clever move, Miss Maynesfield, I credit you that,' he laughed in a faintly embarrassed way.

'What about it, Mr Ramdhuni?' she pressed home her point. 'Don't you think that the children who will be living in these houses are entitled to the same privileges your children enjoy?'

He leaned back in his chair, his fingers laced across his chest and a thoughtful smile on his lips, then he sat up and nodded abruptly. 'You have convinced me. Make the alterations you have suggested, and let me know as soon as the plans are ready.'

Victory was a sweet sensation Sarika had never experienced before. It raced along her bloodstream to create an excitement all its own, and she hastily rolled up the plans and returned the rest of her papers to her briefcase.

'Thank you for your time, Mr Ramdhuni,' she smiled, and they shook hands across his desk.

'It's been a pleasure doing business with you, Miss Maynesfield,' he assured her, coming round his desk to see her to the door.

It was a minute to one when she stepped out of the building, and a few seconds later Sean pulled up beside her in his hired Mercedes. They drove to a small restaurant Sarika had discovered on a previous visit, and it was only when they sat facing each other across the small circular table that Sean broached the subject of her meeting with Mr Ramdhuni.

'Was your meeting fruitful?'

'Mr Ramdhuni didn't like my ideas at first,' she grimaced. 'You can't westernise the East, Miss Maynesfield,' she mimicked Mr Ramdhuni's mannerisms and accent to perfection, and Sean shook with silent laughter.

'What made him agree to it in the end?'

'I more or less tricked him into it,' she confessed, explaining what had occurred. 'It was sheer luck for me, of course, that there happened to be a park near his home.'

Their conversation was interruped when the waiter brought them the menu and they both ordered a light lunch.

'Did you have much success with the client you had to meet?' Sarika questioned Sean the moment they were alone again.

'I clinched a deal for a new school that has to be erected here in Agra,' he explained the reason for his visit to the city.

'We ought to celebrate, considering that we've both had a successful morning,' she suggested lightly, and his dark eyes glittered with devilish laughter when he leaned towards her across the table.

'Dare we order a bottle of wine?'

'Let's,' she agreed with a hint of conspiracy in her soft, triumphant laughter.

Sean beckoned the steward and ordered a bottle of their best wine. It was brought to their table some minutes later, and they toasted each other on their success.

Sarika felt herself relaxing with Sean for the first time since they had met. Sean, too, seemed more at ease, and she could understand now why Jaishree and her family had found him such pleasant and interesting company. The wine also set the mood, and after one glass she had lowered her guard considerably.

'Am I right in thinking it was me you wanted to take out to dinner last night?' she asked before she could stop herself, and Sean smiled twistedly.

'That was a clever guess, honey.'

'I'm sorry.'

'It worked out for the best,' he said in a clipped voice. 'It doesn't always pay to become too friendly with one's associates in business, and the way things are between you and me we might have ended the evening with a flaming row.'

'You're probably right,' she laughed, but inside she felt oddly like crying.

'Shall we take that drive out to the Taj Mahal?' Sean queried when they had finished off their meal with a cup of coffee.

'If you want to,' she agreed, 'and if there's still time.'

'We have enough time,' he assured her, glancing at his watch. 'Let's go.'

He settled the bill and they drove out to the Taj Mahal on the south bank of the Jumna river. Sarika had been there several times before, but each visit was like a new experience. The white marble mausoleum, with its balloon-shaped dome, minarets and corner pavilions, seemed to float majestically above the tree-lined reflecting pools. It dazzled Sarika's eyes in the sunlight as they walked towards it along the edge of the pool.

Sarika did not speak, and neither did Sean. His hand brushed against hers, and somehow their fingers clung as they walked on in silence. The building dwarfed them at close proximity, and Sarika stared up at it in awe and renewed fascination as she studied the walls which were decorated with inlaid flowers in semi-precious stones. Sean was also impressed, but Sarika could not gauge whether his interest was of an architectural or personal nature. When they walked away from it a half hour later, she glanced back across the deserted gardens to see the magnificent building etched against the clear blue sky.

'Isn't it beautiful and peaceful here?' she whispered, and Sean nodded without speaking.

'The mausoleum was built during the years 1632 to 1649 by the Mughal emperor Shah Jahan,' she quietly related the history of the Taj Mahal to Sean. 'The Shah had it built in memory of his wife he had loved so much. Mumtaz Mahal had unfortunately died in childbirth after being his inseparable companion for nineteen years.' Her eyes filled with tears as she felt the pain of that lost love as if it were her own. 'Did you know,' she added in a choked voice, 'that he had her coffin placed in such a way in the mausoleum that the rays of the full moon would always penetrate the opening in the roof to bathe her coffin in its heavenly light?' She felt Sean turn towards her curiously, and she averted her eyes hastily to hide her tears, but . . . too late. He drew her towards a bench and pulled her down beside him, offering her his handkerchief. 'It's so terribly sad, and it always makes me cry,' she explained with an embarrassed laugh.

'You're an incredible mixture,' he chuckled, sliding an arm about her shoulders so that she was forced to lean her head against him. 'What happened to the Shah?' he prompted.

'He was imprisoned by his power-hungry son in Agra's Red Fort, and when Shah Jahan lay dying he had a mirror placed on the ceiling so that he could still see the magnificent monument he had had built for his wife.' She sniffed into the fine linen to control her tears. 'Isn't that beautiful?'

'My God, you're as soft as a kitten really, but I've also seen you with your claws unsheathed like a wildcat. Right now you smell like the fragile petals of the wild jasmine, and I wonder what surprises you still have in store for me.'

'Don't mock me,' she begged, giving him back his handkerchief and intensely aware of that strong arm clamped about her shoulders.

'Would I mock you on such a lovely day, and in such

a beautiful place?' he asked, tilting her face up to his with his strong fingers.

She had expected to see that familiar glint of mockery in his eyes despite his denial, but there was none. There was, however, something in the way he looked at her that made that tell-tale pulse at the base of her throat beat fast and erratically. His chiselled, often stern mouth curved in a sensuous smile, then his features blurred, and she closed her eyes as his mouth touched hers. It could have been the two glasses of wine she had consumed with her lunch, or it could be that she was being affected by the strange enchantment of the Taj Mahal and its history. Sarika could not decide which, but her lips parted invitingly beneath Sean's, and her hand slid up across his chest until her fingers came to rest at the nape of his strong neck where his hair touched the collar of his jacket.

Sean's arm tightened about her shoulders, and she felt his hand slide inside the short-sleeved jacket of her pale blue suit. His touch was warm against her waist through the cotton of her blouse, and it was then that something incredible and wonderful began to stir inside her. At any other time she might have suppressed that feeling, but her resistance was low at that moment, and that incredible feeling persisted until she could not ignore the inevitable truth. She was in love with Sean.

He raised his head the next instant and, as their arms fell away from each other, she wondered a little nervously whether he had sensed the change in her, but his expression was shuttered as he got to his feet and pulled her up with him.

'It's time to go,' he said abruptly, and they walked back to where he had parked the car without touching each other.

He was suddenly so distant that it felt as if she had been thrust out into the cold, and resentment stormed through her. How dared he behave as if nothing had happened, while she . . . oh, God, she had been a fool! She had fallen in love with a man who had no need of her; a man who would soon be leaving Bombay to pursue his business and personal activities elsewhere, and she would be forgotten until circumstances might force him to favour them at some future date with his presence at the Apex company.

Sarika's anger rose, but it was an anger directed at herself, and she lapsed into a silence which Sean did not attempt to break. He also did not question it, and Sarika was left with the humiliating belief that he had guessed her feelings. His cold and aloof manner was apparently his way of telling her that she had overstepped the mark. He was a free agent; he came and went as he pleased and, knowing his reconceived opinion of her, she was left with the despairing knowledge that she would never stand a chance.

Jaishree's wedding created a welcome diversion at the end of two weeks which had been mentally and emotionally trying for Sarika. Dressed for the occasion that Saturday evening in a wine-red sari, Sarika stepped up to the full-length mirror to study herself critically. A fine gold thread had been hand-woven in an elaborate pattern into the six yards of fine silk, and it was draped about her tall, slender body in true Hindu style. Her hair was brushed away from her face to hang in a heavy plait down her back, and behind her Ayah stood nodding approvingly.

'You have never looked more beautiful, *pyaari*,' Ayah smiled at her warmly, 'and I am proud of you.'

Sarika smiled back at her and turned to collect the gaily wrapped parcel on her bed. She had bought a damask tablecloth in England as a gift for her mother, and she could not think of anyone she would rather gave it to than Jaishree.

Sean was pacing the hall like a caged tiger when Sarika and Ayah went downstairs, but he halted abruptly when he heard their voices, and he turned to glance up at them when they were descending the last few steps. His dark suit enhanced his rugged good looks, and Sarika's heart missed a couple of beats when his glance flicked over her, but, as always, she was left with that cold feeling that he had weighed her and found her wanting.

'Does Sarika not look beautiful?' Ayah questioned him innocently when they reached his side, and this time his dark gaze seemed to smoulder with derisive mockery when it slid over Sarika.

'Sarika doesn't need me to tell her that she's beautiful, Ayah. I'm sure her mirror has done that quite convincingly.'

Ayah laughed happily, unaware of the sting behind those words, but Sarika felt the blood rush to her cheeks and recede again to leave her pale and shaken. She lowered her lashes hastily to hide the shadow of pain in her eyes, but Sean had already turned away to open the door and usher them out to the Land Rover parked in the driveway.

Attending Jaishree's wedding was also an unexpected reunion of old friends. Melissa Armstrong was there with Craig Jenkins, and Michael Nicholson was there, of course, with Stephen and Claudia. There was time only to introduce Sean and to exchange a few words with them all before they had to enter the hall where a number of guests had already seated themselves. Sarika and Sean left their gifts on the table when they arrived, and they were told to go up on to the stage where seating had been provided for family and close friends. Ayah led the way and, to Sarika's dismay, she found herself seated alone with Sean while Ayah joined a group of acquaintances at the opposite end of the stage. Stephen, Claudia, and Michael had followed them up on to the stage, and Sarika was uncomfortably sandwiched in between Michael and Sean.

'You look lovely this evening,' Michael whispered to her, his smile warm, and his appreciative glance darting all over her.

Sarika murmured something appropriate, but she could not recall later what it had been. She was too aware of Sean's muscular thigh pressed against her own, and the unnerving sensation she experienced each time his shoulder brushed against hers. She was so near to Sean, and yet so far, she realised, and she looked straight ahead of her without seeing anything until she had succeeded in controlling that surge of painful longing inside her.

Her glance shifted slowly down into the hall. The women were dripping with jewellery and resplendent in their colourful saris. It was as if they were competing with each other for the honour of being chosen the best dressed Indian woman present, and Sarika felt plain in comparison. The men wore evening suits, and a few wore well-cut evening jackets with their *dhotis*, but no matter how distinguished they looked, they were completely outshone by the women.

Recorded music began to fill the hall. It was the lilting, haunting music of the East played on the sitar, and for one poignant moment Sarika was transported back to that afternoon at the Taj Mahal. She felt again the magic and the mystery, and that forbidden warmth which had suffused her entire being. It lasted no more than a brief moment, then she thrust it from her mentally as one might thrust aside a sinful thought with self-disgust.

She tried to relax her tightly clenched hands and allowed her glance to slide over the stage which was elaborately decorated with flowers and brightly painted arches which had been sprinkled with gold glitter. It looked festive despite the solemnity of the occasion, and it was in this colourful setting that the bridegroom sat with his best man while they awaited the arrival of the priest and the bride.

She felt the pressure of Sean's shoulder increase against hers, and turned her head to see him glancing down at her enquiringly. 'I understood there was more to a Hindu wedding than this one ceremony.'

'Oh, but there is,' she answered him in a lowered voice. 'Two or three days before the wedding there's the

Sanjee, a fun party, to which guests from both families are invited, with the exception of the groom. The bride is teased quite a bit about her forthcoming status, and the women dance the *garba*, which is the national folk dance. On the morning of the actual wedding day they have the *Mandwa*, to which only guests from the bride's side are invited. The priest says a prayer, the solemn part of this ceremony is dealt with, and then the fun begins. The young married women are required to rub turmeric powder mixed with olive oil on the bride, and they may rub it on her wherever they wish. The older generation believe that this mixture rubbed on the bride improves her complexion so that she'll look radiant at the wedding ceremony.'

'It sounds fascinating,' he murmured, and Sarika could see for once that he really meant it.

The elaborate ceremony was about to begin. The sitar music was toned down to play softly in the background, and a hushed silence fell on the guests as the priest stepped out on to the stage in his yellow robe with its red and gold border down the front and along the bottom of the long garment. The edges of the sleeves were trimmed with the same border, and on his head he wore a white, two-pointed hat made of cotton with adequate stiffening on the inside which was similar to that which the bridegroom was wearing. The priest recited a short prayer with the barefooted bridegroom, then a sheet was raised like a partition to prevent the groom witnessing the bride's arrival.

'Jaishree is going to be called out on to the stage,' Sarika explained softly to Sean. 'She's not allowed to see Vinod, and he's not allowed to see her until a second ceremony is performed.'

Even as she spoke she could hear the tinkle of the little bells attached to the ankle chains which every Hindu bride wore, and a moment later Jaishree stepped on to the stage accompanied by her father. She was dressed in traditional Hindu fashion with gold jewellery hanging about her throat and dripping from her wrists and fingers. Flowers had been plaited into her hair, and her radiance, Sarika suspected, had nothing to do with the turmeric powder and olive oil which had been rubbed on her that morning. Sarika felt the sting of tears behind her eyelids, and a pang of inexplicable envy, but she suppressed both fiercely.

'It's customary for the bride to wear two saris on her wedding day,' said Sarika, aware at the same time that Michael was glancing at her oddly from time to time. 'The red and green sari is from Jaishree's side of the family, and the white and red from Vinod's side. Both are, of course, hand-embroidered with a twenty-two-carat gold thread, and they're both draped in such a way that the one sari is on the left side of her body, and the other on her right.'

Out of the corner of her eye she could see Sean studying her intently, and she turned her head as if drawn by a magnet until their glances met. His eyes glittered strangely, almost mockingly, and she felt herself stiffen.

'Am I boring you with all the details?'

'I knew you would be an informative companion.' The stern mouth relaxed in a suggestion of a smile. 'That's why I didn't object to Ayah joining her friends.'

Dared she take that as a compliment after his cutting remark before they left the house that evening? Sarika did not have time to wonder about it. The priest was performing the second ceremony with the bridegroom, then the partition was removed. Vinod got to his feet, and he and Jaishree exchanged garlands as well as glances which once again sent that unusual stab of envy through Sarika as she watched them sit down facing each other with the container between them in which the fire had been lit.

Halfway through the proceedings Vinod was allowed to sit next to Jaishree, and Sarika, because of her grasp of the language, could explain to Sean most of what was being said. The colourful ceremony took almost two and a half hours, and it ended with Vinod taking

Jaishree's hand while they slowly took the final seven steps together with the priest saying a short prayer with each step they took.

'With every step they're taking a vow. Something like "for richer, for poorer; in sickness and in health", and so on,' Sarika explained with an extraordinary lump in her throat, and the lilting music plucked from the sitar rose above the excited voices of the guests and tugged painfully at her soul.

CHAPTER EIGHT

FLOWER petals rained on the bride and groom at the end of the wedding ceremony, and the family gathered around to wish them well. It was only when they had moved on to the adjoining hall that Sean and Sarika had the opportunity to approach Jaishree and her husband.

Sean spoke to them, and, for a man who did not believe in marriage, he voiced his wishes for their future happiness with a sincerity that puzzled Sarika as she took a handful of flower petals from the tray held out to her. She showered it on the bridal couple, and joined hands with them.

'I'm so happy for you both,' she said and, too choked to say more, kissed Vinod's cheek and embraced her friend.

'Thank you, Sarika,' Jaishree smiled with that special radiance which had not wavered once during the lengthy ceremony. 'I hope you and Mr O'Connor will stay and join us for the meal which has been prepared?'

'We shall be delighted,' Sean answered for Sarika, taking her arm and leading her off the stage into the adjoining hall where trestle tables laden with food awaited the hungry guests.

'Shall we all sit together?' asked Michael, coming up alongside them with his parents directly behind him, and Sarika shot a questioning glance at Sean.

His granite-hard features and dark, unfathomable eyes gave her no indication how he felt about Michael's suggestion, and, to fill the awkward silence which was erupting, she said hastily, 'That would be a good idea.'

Sean released his grip on her arm, and she somehow sensed his annoyance even though his features revealed nothing. Seated beside Michael, with Sean, Claudia and

Stephen facing them, Sarika was confronted with Sean's rugged good looks for the second time that evening, and something inside her twisted into an aching knot.

'At last I'm going to have an opportunity to talk to you,' Michael succeeded in capturing her attention, and she dragged her gaze from Sean to look into Michael's grey, accusing eyes. 'You were so busy explaining the wedding ritual to Mr O'Connor that I couldn't get a word in edgeways.'

Sarika felt a twinge of guilt. 'I'm sorry if it seemed as if I was ignoring you.'

'You look so beautiful this evening that I'll forgive you anything,' he accepted her apology with an unmistakable warmth in his eyes, and she smiled at him with a coquetry born of despair.

'Why, thank you,' she said, but she could have kicked herself afterwards when she realised that Michael had taken her behaviour as encouragement to strike up a flirtation with her.

Across the table Sean's glance met hers occasionally, and his dark eyes glittered with a crushing mockery that robbed Sarika of her appetite. She played with her food instead of eating it, and tried to concentrate on the conversation she was having with Michael, but her glance went repeatedly to Sean, who was involved in a lengthy discussion with Claudia and Stephen. There was something about him that evening that made it impossible for her to keep her eyes off him, and despite the fact that she was occupied with Michael, there was a part of her which was listening to every nuance in Sean's deep, gravelly voice.

'When are you coming through to Poona again?' Claudia asked Sarika when there was a lull in the conversation.

'I'm not sure,' Sarika replied, her glance darting nervously in Sean's direction, but his rugged features remained expressionless. 'I've been rather tied up at the office lately,' she added lamely.

'You surely don't work weekends,' protested Claudia, tilting her fair head at Sarika enquiringly.

'No, I don't, but——'

'Then what about coming through next week Saturday and spending the weekend with us?' Claudia interrupted, and before Sarika could reply, the older woman had turned to smile at Sean. 'You're welcome to come as well, Mr O'Connor. If you like riding you'll find we have a couple of excellent horses in our stables.'

'Your invitation is tempting, but I'm afraid I shan't be here,' he declined, and the noise in the hall seemed to rise to a crescendo as Sean added: 'I'm flying to Australia this coming Monday, and I have no idea when I'll be back.'

It felt oddly as if the bottom had fallen out of Sarika's world, and there was an accusation in her tawny eyes when she managed to capture his glance. 'You didn't tell me you were planning a trip to Australia.'

Sean smiled at her with a tolerance one would adopt with a child. 'I received a call from my office in Brisbane late this afternoon, and you know as well as I do that we haven't actually had the opportunity to talk until now.'

'Are you permanently stationed in Australia, Mr O'Connor?' Claudia intervened on what could have been an explosive moment, and Sean turned to her at once.

'No, ma'am,' he smiled briefly at the woman beside him. 'My home, if one could call it that, is in the United States, but I also spend a great deal of time in many other countries.'

'And what about your wife?' probed Claudia in a way that made Sarika hold her breath. 'Is she happy with the fact that you're away from home for such lengthy periods at a time?'

'I don't have a wife, ma'am,' Sean replied smoothly. 'In my kind of job a wife would be nothing but a nuisance.'

Sarika felt as if she had been hovering precariously on a high building and had suddenly been pushed over the edge. Her insides jolted sickeningly, and out of the mist that clouded her mind came Michael's reproachful voice.

'Sarika, you aren't listening!'

'I'm sorry.' She made a valiant effort to pull herself together. 'What were you saying?'

'I'm coming through to Bombay on Monday, and I'm staying until Friday,' he enlightened her, and she grasped blindly at this information to steady herself.

'Then you must come to dinner one evening,' she said on the spur of the moment, and Michael smiled at her broadly.

'I was hoping you'd invite me.'

Sarika could not remember much of what happened afterwards. She was aware of talking to Michael, but she could not recall what she had said. Across the table Sean's eyes mocked and chided her alternately, and she was inordinately relieved when Ayah beckoned from across the hall that it was time to leave. Sarika had time to say a brief farewell to Jaishree and Vinod, and when they were leaving she felt a hand touch her lightly on the arm.

'I'll be in touch,' Melissa Armstrong promised when Sarika turned to face her, and Sarika forced her stiff lips into a smile of acknowledgement before she was whisked out of the hall.

Sarika sat in front with Sean when they drove home, but it was Ayah, seated in the back, who filled what might have been a strained silence with her excited, almost monologic conversation until they arrived at the house. Sean garaged the Land Rover, and when they entered the house Ayah excused herself immediately and went to her room. Sarika wanted to do the same, but she had barely walked a few paces towards the stairs when strong fingers snaked about her wrist.

'Have a drink with me before you go up to bed?'

A polite refusal hovered on her lips, but when she

looked up into Sean's rugged face she found herself accepting his invitation, and she wondered frantically whether he could feel the acceleration of her pulse rate where his fingers rested against her wrist.

He released her in the living-room and she lowered herself into a chair, arranging her sari about her legs while he walked across to the cabinet to pour a whisky for himself and a sherry for her. She knew she was staring at him, but she could not help it. Her glance lingered on the back of his dark head and the wide shoulders beneath the evening jacket, and an aching longing stirred deep inside of her which she hastily suppressed when he turned towards her. She accepted the glass of sherry from him in silence, and he seated himself in the chair close to hers with his long legs stretched out characteristically in front of him.

'I want to thank you for explaining so much to me at the wedding ceremony this evening,' he severed the silence between them.

'It was a pleasure,' she murmured politely, sipping at her sherry, and hoping he did not notice the slight tremor in her hand.

'The Nicholsons are a fine couple, and it's a pity I had to turn down Claudia's invitation.' He loosened his black string tie and undid the top button of his white silk shirt while his dark eyes probed hers. 'Are you going through to Poona next weekend?'

'I might,' she answered evasively, and Sean's eyes filled with mockery.

'I guess you know that Michael is crazy about you.'

The mouthful of sherry turned sour in her mouth, and she swallowed it down hastily. 'I'm going to bed.'

'Sarika!' He held up a deterring hand and she found herself sinking back into her chair, but this time she sat on the edge of it in preparation for flight. 'What's been bugging you these past few days?'

Her heart jolted in her breast. Didn't he know? Hadn't he guessed the secret she had been carrying around with her the past few days? What could she say without making him suspect that he was the cause of her misery she had thought she had hidden so well behind her aloof manner?

'I don't know what you're talking about,' she played for time, lowering her gaze to her hands clasped so tightly in her lap.

'Okay, if you want me to spell it out for you, I will!' he exploded with a harshness that made her flinch inwardly. 'Since the day we went to Agra you've been exceptionally cool and quiet. Explaining the marriage ritual to me was the most you've said to me in days, and then it was only because I imagine you felt obliged to do so.'

Her pulses fluttered nervously. 'You're imagining things.'

'I learnt at a very early age never to rely on my imagination, but to rely instead on cold, hard facts, so don't give me that excuse.'

She was being driven into a corner, and she realised that the only way out was to launch an attack of her own. She squared her shoulders, and raised her head to meet the onslaught of his eyes with a glint of anger in her own. 'All right, so I haven't been very talkative lately, but you've been somewhat cool and distant yourself.'

'I've had a lot on my mind.'

'So have I,' she explained quietly.

Their glances locked for tense, angry seconds, then his rugged features relaxed visibly. 'Okay, I accept that.'

Sarika sighed inwardly with relief and sagged back into her chair as if the strain had been too much for her body. There was still a mouthful of sherry left in her glass, and she swallowed it down in the hope that it would steady the tremors which had erupted inside her.

'How long do you expect to be away?' she broached the subject which had been troubling her since his surprise statement at the reception.

'I don't know,' he shrugged, raising his glass to his lips and draining it. 'A week, maybe more.'

'And what happens to Apex while you're away?'

'You'll have to take over.'

A mixture of incredulity and anger exploded inside her. 'You really meant it when you said that after two weeks you'd throw me in at the deep end!'

'I didn't know then that I wouldn't be here, but I'm convinced you'll manage.'

'Is that a compliment?' she queried cautiously.

'No, honey, it's a fact,' he smiled briefly. 'Miranda will give you all the assistance you need, and I've left a telephone number on the desk in the study in case an emergency crops up which neither of you can handle.'

A wave of anxiety swept through Sarika, and she held out her glass to him. 'I think I'll have another sherry.'

There was a hint of mockery in his eyes when he got up to refill their glasses, and it was with his back turned to her that he asked: 'Does the prospect of taking charge of the company scare you?'

'It terrifies me!' she confessed as he turned and walked back to his chair with a glass in each hand, and the smile in his eyes deepened as he handed her her sherry.

'I give you ten out of ten for honesty,' he told her, 'and that, honey, is a compliment.'

Sarika stared at him thoughtfully when he slumped back into his chair and lit a cheroot. 'I don't suppose you've ever been scared of attempting what appears to be the impossible.'

'I've been scared many times,' he surprised her with his confession, 'but it gets the adrenalin pumping, and that sharpens the brain.'

'I imagine it's the challenge you find so irresistible.'

'And the triumph when I succeed.'

'I can understand that,' she nodded, recalling her own triumph when she had succeeded in convincing Mr Ramdhuni that her ideas for the housing scheme were more practical.

They sat without talking for some time, and it was

not until they had emptied their glasses and Sean had put out his cheroot in the ashtray that Sarika broke the silence between them.

'How long have you been here in Bombay?' she questioned him conversationally, and his eyebrows met in a frown of concentration.

'Seven months, not counting the times I had to go elsewhere.'

'Don't you miss your home?' she asked, thinking about her own unhappiness when she had been away from home for a lengthy period.

'Home is an apartment in Manhattan,' Sean laughed shortly, 'and there's nothing and no one to miss.'

Against her will, Sarika recalled his remark to Claudia. 'In my kind of job a wife would be nothing but a nuisance,' he had said, and she felt again that sickening jolt beneath her rib cage.

'Do you honestly intend to spend your life wandering around the world without someone to share it with you, or someone to go home to?' she heard herself asking, and she could have bitten off her tongue the next instant when his mouth curved in a derisive smile.

'If you've caught the wedding fever, then I suggest you spread your tentacles in Michael's direction, not mine.'

'Dammit, you know I didn't mean——' She broke off abruptly, realising there was some truth in what he had said, and her cheeks became suffused with colour and she got angrily to her feet. 'Forget it!'

'Just a moment!' He had moved with an incredible speed to halt her flight from the room and, standing in front of her, he raised a hand to her hair and withdrew it a second later with a pink rose petal between his fingers. 'Put this under your pillow, honey, and you might dream of the man you'll marry some day, who knows.'

His mockery was more than she could cope with at that moment. It sliced deep and painfully, and she glared up at him with the fury of a wounded animal. 'Go to the devil, Sean O'Connor!'

She pushed past him and stormed up to her room, but his mocking laughter echoed in her mind long after she had gone to bed and put out the light. *Fool*, she cursed herself. *Idiot!* But nothing could alleviate that feeling of utter despair.

Sarika leaned back in her chair and sighed. Her desk was cluttered with plans, files, and correspondence which she still had to read through and answer. The head of the drawing department had spent more than an hour with her that morning because they were having problems with the plans being drawn up for an extension to a factory, the chief accountant was in a rage because one of his staff had made an incorrect entry in one of the books, the chief of personnel refused to fire the man for what he considered a justifiable error, and three surveyors trooped into her office with the complaint that they were encountering difficulties in their survey of a piece of land. Added to this the telephone never seemed to stop ringing all day, and Sarika was not always sure what to deal with first.

'Is it always this busy, or am I simply finding it difficult coping with my own work as well as Sean's?' she asked Miranda when she came in with a batch of letters that needed Sarika's signature.

'This is one of the worst days I've known in years,' Miranda enlightened her with a sympathetic smile.

'Thank God for that!' sighed Sarika, drawing the letters towards her and attaching her signature at the bottom of each.

'It's time to go home,' Miranda announced when Sarika had signed the last letter.

'Is it that late?' Sarika glanced at her watch and discovered to her dismay that it was long after five. 'I'm sorry, Miranda, I didn't mean to keep you.'

'It's not your fault,' the older woman assured her. 'I was rather bogged down with work myself today, and

I'm looking forward to a quiet evening at home to help me unwind.'

'I echo that,' laughed Sarika, clearing her desk hastily before she left the office.

Her quiet evening at home was not quite as she had hoped it would be. She had imagined that, without Sean's disturbing presence, she would recapture some of the good times she had had alone with Ayah when her parents had been away, but instead a feeling of desolation gripped her, and she could not shake it off.

'You are missing Sean, are you not, *pyaari*?' Ayah put Sarika's feelings into words when they were midway through the evening meal, and for a startled second Sarika almost agreed with Ayah.

'I don't miss him at all,' she denied her own feelings with a wariness she had applied since childhood.

'I have cared for you since the day you were born. Do you think I am unaware of the feelings you take such care to hide?' Velvet brown eyes smiled at Sarika with a tender warmth. 'I know you too well, *beti*.'

Sarika sat there tense and nervous, as if the walls had ears to hear and lips to reveal what was being said. 'If you mention anything to Sean about——'

'It is not for me to say anything,' Ayah interrupted calmly. 'It is for you to open the doors of your heart and to let the truth spill from your lips, but I am afraid you have thrown away the key.'

'Are you lecturing me?' Sarika tried to make light of what Ayah had said.

'I am not lecturing you,' Ayah shook her head, 'but I pray that I shall live to see the day that key is found. You are living behind the closed doors of your heart, Sarika, because you are afraid, but it is a lonely life, and I would not want you to end your days in self-imposed exile.'

Self-imposed exile! The words hammered against her brain until every other thought was driven away. Was that what she was doing to herself?

Sarika did not have much time to ponder the

thought. Michael arrived some minutes later, and Ayah's remark was almost totally forgotten for the rest of that evening.

'Are you annoyed with me?' Michael asked when the hands of the grandfather clock were reaching towards eleven, and Sarika glanced at him in surprise.

'Why on earth should I be annoyed with you?'

'I've just realised that you've been very quiet, and I'm the one who's been doing all the talking this evening.'

A faintly mocking smile curved her wide, sensitive mouth. 'That proves I'm a good listener.'

'Or that you've been thinking about something else . . . or someone.'

Sarika's insides lurched uncomfortably. Was he perhaps referring to Sean? She dismissed the thought at once. 'I've had rather a hectic day, and I'm tired, but I've enjoyed listening to you.'

'If you had told me you were tired I would have left long ago,' Michael frowned, and he would have got up to leave if she had not placed a detaining hand on his arm.

'Now you're offended, and I didn't mean it that way,' she explained. 'I'm glad you came because I know I couldn't have tolerated being alone this evening.'

'Do you miss him that much?'

Sarika's body stiffened. This time she could not dismiss Michael's remark and pretend that she did not know what he was referring to.

'If you mean Sean O'Connor, then you're mistaken.' After the lecture Ayah had given her she found herself denying her feelings with a twinge of discomfort, but she continued to do so nevertheless. 'I don't miss him at all, and it's heaven, in fact, to have the house to myself for a change.'

Michael's grey eyes had studied her intently while she spoke, then he looked away. 'If he travels about as much as he implied the other night, then I imagine you'll have the house to yourself more often in the future.'

'Yes, I suppose I shall.'

She should have felt elated, but instead the thought depressed her. Without Sean's dynamic and vital presence in the house she might just as well be living in a morgue, and a little shiver raced up her spine to leave her feeling cold.

Michael kissed her lightly on the cheek a few minutes later, and left. He had filled the empty hours for her, but he was not Sean, she realised when she went up to bed. Sean somehow made his presence felt in the house, and Sarika always knew he was there even though they did not often spend time together. When they were together, however, they nearly always argued, and she wished it did not have to be so.

She put out the light and tried to think of Michael rather than Sean, but Michael's handsome, youthful features repeatedly made way for Sean's rugged male looks. Her thoughts wandered to that afternoon at the Taj Mahal. She felt again his lips against hers and the touch of his hands, but Sean had remained cool and unaffected while the longing had burned deep inside her. For him it was no more than a game, but for her it had become the very essence of her existence.

'Hell!' she muttered fiercely, pounding her pillow with her fist and wishing it could have been Sean's mocking features at the receiving end. Her anger died swiftly, however, and she turned her face into the pillow. 'Sean . . . oh, Sean!' she whispered his name in despair.

Sarika was determined not to give herself time to think about Sean. During the rest of that week she was kept busy at the office, but never quite as busy as she had been on the Monday, and most of her evenings were spent with Michael. He came to dinner once, but they dined out during the remainder of that week, and Sarika could not help but be aware of Ayah's displeasure.

'Come through to Poona with me tomorrow morning,' Michael suggested the Friday afternoon when he telephoned her at the office, but Sarika was hesitant to agree.

'I'll think about it and let you know this evening,' she promised.

She had almost made up her mind not to go when she arrived home late that afternoon to find a letter addressed to Sean lying on the table in the hall. The letter had been sent from New York, and the handwriting was definitely feminine. Could it be from one of those many women in his past? she wondered cynically, but the thought sent a stab of jealousy through her. It was this that made her decide to go to Poona with Michael for the weekend. She desperately needed to get her life back into perspective, but most of all she needed something to make her forget these futile longings churning through her.

The weekend at Poona with the Nicholsons was peaceful and relaxing after the hectic week at the office without Sean. Michael was attentive and charming, but at the oddest times Sarika found herself thinking about Sean and wondering what he was doing. She would banish him at once from her mind, but she never quite succeeded in banishing him entirely. She had hoped the weekend away from home would help her come to terms with herself and her bleak-looking future, but she had failed in her attempts to shake off that black cloud of despair under which she was labouring.

Michael drove her home the Sunday evening, and he was strangely quiet behind the wheel of his Porsche, but on the outskirts of Bombay he pulled off the road and switched on the roof light before he turned to face her.

'There's something I must tell you.' He took her hands in his and she knew somehow what he was going to say, but when she tried to stop him he said quickly, 'No, don't interrupt me, Sarika. This is something I have to get off my chest.' He stared for some time at her hands resting in his, then he raised his glance, and the graveness of his expression almost frightened her. 'I know I'm falling in love with you, but I also know I don't stand a chance.'

'Oh, Michael!' she whispered, guilt and remorse blending as his words fell like painful darts on her conscience.

'You're in love with Sean O'Connor.'

Sarika felt as if she had been struck by a bolt of lightning, and her face paled. 'You don't know what you're saying!'

'I suspected it the night of Jaishree's wedding, but I'm sure of it now.'

'No!' she protested, trying to wrench her hands from his as a wave of panic washed over her, but Michael's fingers tightened their grip on hers.

'I've seen the way you look at him, Sarika, and you may not be aware of it, but you brought his name into nearly every conversation you had with me and my parents this weekend.'

She shook her head in bewilderment and disbelief. 'I couldn't have!'

'Sarika, look at me!' He released her hands to tilt up her chin, and she was forced to meet his eyes. 'You love him, don't you.'

It was a statement, not a query, and for the second time she felt the shock of it rippling through her. She had been aware of her feelings for Sean, but when Michael put it into words he made it a stark reality, and the pain it inflicted was almost unbearable. He was waiting for her to say something, but she stared at him mutely and momentarily incapable of speech.

He released her abruptly and turned from her to grip the steering wheel with his hands. 'Never mind, you don't have to say anything. It's there in your eyes, and if Sean O'Connor has any sense——'

He broke off abruptly, and he was clenching the wheel so tightly that she was afraid it might snap in his hands. Remorse and guilt surged through her again, and she touched his sleeve tentatively. 'I'm sorry, Michael.'

'Don't apologise, Sarika.' His smile was a little twisted when he reached for her hand unexpectedly and raised it to his lips. 'You aren't to blame for the way I feel.'

They travelled the rest of the way in silence, and it was ten o'clock when Michael followed her into the living-room and placed her overnight bag on the floor beside a chair. Sarika felt awkward. Michael might not consider her to blame for the way he felt, but she blamed herself entirely for encouraging a relationship which she had known from the start would not mean as much to her as it would to him. She wanted to say something to relieve the tension between them, but she was too unhappy at that moment to think of anything.

'We can still be friends, can't we?' Michael broke the silence between them and, taking her by the shoulders, he turned her to face him.

'Do you think that would be wise?' she asked cautiously, not wanting to hurt him more than she had hurt him already.

'I'd like to be there if you should need me.'

'Oh, Michael!' she smiled shakily at his quietly spoken statement. 'Thank you.'

He drew her towards him gently, and she did not protest when he pressed his lips to hers in an almost brotherly salute.

'Am I interrupting something?' A deep, mocking voice made them draw apart as if they had been indulging in something which was forbidden, and Sarika spun round to face the man who stood leaning against the door jamb with the thumb of one hand hooked into his belt and a cheroot smouldering between the fingers of the other.

'Sean!' His name spilled from her lips in a mixture of delight and fear. 'I never expected you back so soon.'

His derisive gaze flicked over her briefly before it settled on Michael. 'I presume Sarika spent the weekend at your home in Poona?'

'That's correct, Mr O'Connor,' Michael answered politely, his grey glance darting curiously at Sarika.

'Thank you for bringing her home safely, and pass on my regards to your parents,' Sean was saying, and Sarika felt embarrassingly that he was making it clear he had no wish to extend his hospitality towards Michael.

'I'll do that,' said Michael, shifting his weight on his feet in obvious discomfort as he glanced briefly at Sarika. 'I'll call you some time.'

The silence in the room was incredibly tense after Michael had left, and Sarika steeled herself automatically when Sean sauntered towards her. In black slacks and sweat-shirt he looked dark and dangerous, and the glittering harshness in his eyes did not promise a pleasant confrontation.

'It appears you've succeeded in leading Michael up the garden path,' he smiled contemptuously. 'May I know how soon you intend to lead him up the aisle?'

Sarika felt that storm of anger rise within her which only Sean could arouse, but she forced herself to remain outwardly calm. 'That's none of your business, surely?'

'I'm making it my damn business!' he said through his teeth as he crushed his cheroot into an ashtray and lessened the distance between them to tower over her. 'I'm a lot older than he is, I've seen the way women like you operate, and I'm not going to sit back and watch you lead that young man on, only to drop him later when it suits you.'

She drew a sharp breath as if he had struck her, and her face went white. Dear God, did he always have to hurt her this way? Did he honestly have such a low opinion of her?

'It obviously gives you a great deal of satisfaction and pleasure to hurt and insult me, and I'm not going to do or say anything to deprive you of that.' Her voice was remarkably calm despite the painful turbulence inside her. 'What I would like to know is why do you feel this way? What have I ever done to you, or to anyone else for that matter, that you should have such a low opinion of me?'

He was so close to her that she could smell his particular brand of aftershave. It stirred her senses, but that harsh, twisted smile about his mouth stabbed like ice at her heart.

'You're a woman,' he said, 'and all women possess a calculating and devious streak that makes them flaunt themselves at unsupecting males like Michael. You've also been spoilt, honey,' he added disdainfully. 'During your final year at university you wanted to drop out. It didn't matter to you that your father had spent a lot of money on your studies. You were ready to throw it away, and you had the audacity to demand more to indulge in a venture which gave no guarantee that it would succeed.'

Sarika's head shot up. 'Did my father tell you that?'

'You're damn right he did!'

'I don't suppose you'd believe me if I said he didn't quite tell you the truth?' she probed tentatively.

'You can bet your life I wouldn't believe you!' he snarled, and she lowered her long gold lashes to veil the pain in her eyes.

She felt defeated, beaten, and the pain of it was like a heated blade piercing her soul. How could she tell him? How could she ever tell anyone the true facts? No one would ever believe her . . . least of all Sean!

She turned from him in silence and, picking up her overnight bag, walked out of the living-room with her head held high to hide her feelings. She went up the stairs to her room, but her steps were heavy and laboured as if she was carrying an unaccustomed load on her shoulders.

CHAPTER NINE

THE bathroom walls seemed to fling Sarika's painful thoughts back at her as if they were rubber balls being bounced against the white tiles. There was anger, resentment and despair surging through her, and she winced anew at the pain Sean had inflicted. She was in love with him, it was true, but her lips were unfamiliar with the words, and she could not even say them to herself as she stared at her reflection in the mirror above the hand basin. Her face looked pinched and pale beneath her newly acquired tan, and she pushed a tired hand through her hair as she turned away to open the door into her bedroom.

The bedside light filled the room with its soft glow, and she walked barefoot across the carpet with her head bent while she fastened the belt of her robe, but the next instant she froze, her glance darting wildly about the room when something warned her she was not alone. Sean was seated in an armchair in front of the window, his legs stretched out in front of him, and his arms crossed over his wide chest. His dark glance swept over her with something close to insolence, and an icy anger shook through her.

'What are you doing here in my room?' she demanded, her hands shaking when she tightened the belt of her robe about her waist. 'What do you want?'

'What is the truth, Sarika?' he asked in a quiet, ominous voice, and she did not venture closer to him, but she wondered at the reason for this sudden desire for the truth when less than an hour ago he had been convinced that he knew it.

'The truth is whatever you want to believe,' she answered coldly. 'Now, if you don't mind, I'm tired and I'd like to go to bed.'

Sean made no attempt to leave, and there was a challenge in his piercing glance. 'You can go to bed when I've had a few straight answers.'

'Now look here, Sean,' she stormed at him in a sudden burst of temper, 'this entire house may belong to you, but this happens to be my bedroom, and I want you to get out!'

'Well, at last I'm getting a positive reaction instead of that calm acceptance you displayed downstairs,' he drawled as he got to his feet, and if her anger could have been charted, it would have started a steep climb at that precise moment.

'What the *hell* do you want with me?' she demanded in a voice that shook with fury as he walked towards her. 'You accuse me of leading Michael on only to drop him later, you accuse me of being calculating and devious and of flaunting myself at unsuspecting males, and you give me a lengthy explanation as to why you consider me spoilt. You've sat in judgment on my character, and you've come up with the verdict, so what more do you want! Blood?'

'I want you to defend yourself.'

'Defend myself?' she almost shouted incredulously. 'Why should I want to defend myself when you've already decided what you choose to believe?'

Sean hooked his thumbs into the belt hugging his black slacks to his lean hips, and there was something about his stance that was beginning to frighten her. 'During the past weeks at the office I've seen you fight for what you believe is right or wrong, but when it becomes a personal matter you shut up tighter than a clam, as if you're afraid to let anyone see the real you.'

'I refuse to bare my soul to you or anyone else,' she said coldly, and his jaw hardened with anger.

'I want the truth, Sarika!' he insisted, his eyes burning down into hers as if they wanted to drag the truth from her physically.

'Why this sudden interest now?' she demanded

sarcastically. 'Do you want the added satisfaction of calling me a liar?'

'Sometimes, Sarika, you let your mask slip, and tonight was one of those rare instances.' He looked down into her pale face, his eyes probing hers relentlessly. 'Regardless of what you may think, I don't enjoy hurting you, but I admit that I have deliberately goaded you at times to get to the bottom of a mystery which has been puzzling me since the day I met you at the airport.'

This unexpected revelation drained her of her anger, but it left her wary. There were certain things locked away inside her that she could never tell anyone. Least of all Sean. She did not want his sympathy, and she doubted if she would ever have his understanding.

'There's no mystery that I know of,' she brushed aside his statement, but she could no longer sustain his glance for fear of what he might see.

'We'll let that pass for the moment,' he said abruptly, 'but tell me about the time you wanted to drop out of university.'

Sarika felt her legs trembling beneath her, and an overwhelming tiredness made her step back and sit down heavily on the bed. 'I never wanted to drop out of university,' the confession was dragged from her. 'I had every intention of completing my studies, but I'd become interested in fashion, and I fancied starting a boutique here in Bombay which would sell saris as well as the latest fashions. It was to be my first step towards becoming independent, and towards being accepted as someone in my own right. I asked my father to help me financially with the initial layout. It was to be a loan, but he refused his help, and that was the end of that dream.'

'By that time, I guess, he wasn't in a financial position to help you.' Sean surprised her by accepting her explanation.

'Perhaps,' she shrugged tiredly.

'What's that supposed to mean?'

A sudden wariness drove her to her feet and away from Sean to stand with her slim, straight back turned towards him. 'It means that perhaps my father was in financial difficulties at the time and didn't want to tell me about it, or . . .'

'Go on!' insisted Sean, coming up behind her, and her fingers curled nervously into her palms.

'My father was a man who thought only of himself, and the things that were of personal interest to him and my mother.' The truth was once again torn from her.

'Ah, now we're getting somewhere.'

'We're getting nowhere!' she snapped, angry with herself for having said so much, and intensely aware of Sean standing so close to her that she could almost feel the heat of his body against her back. 'As far as I'm concerned, the subject is closed.'

'You're clamming up on me again, are you?' he accused with a hint of mockery in his voice.

'I have nothing further to say.'

'Sarika . . .' His hands rested on her shoulders, his fingers moving in a strong caress that seemed to massage the tension out of her rigid body, but he was creating a tension of a different nature when he drew her back against his hard body, and her senses responded to the low rumble of his voice close to her ear. 'Don't you trust me?'

'I don't trust anyone,' she said stiffly, aware suddenly that she was wearing nothing but a flimsy nightdress beneath her thin silk robe, and the heat of Sean's body against her own was beginning to awaken emotions she had difficulty in suppressing.

'You're afraid of getting hurt, is that it?'

His accurate guess brought tears to her eyes, and she swallowed down the lump in her throat before she said thickly, 'I don't want to talk about it.'

His fingers ceased their caress, and his hands tightened briefly on her shoulders before he turned her slowly to face him, but she kept her head lowered so that the thick veil of her hair hid those humiliating tears.

'Who did this to you, honey?' Sean asked softly. 'Who hurt you so badly that you can't trust anyone?'

Her body began to tremble beneath his hands, and she could not speak even if she had wanted to. His unexpected understanding and his gentleness were tearing away at her defensive barriers to be replaced by a weakness she knew she would despise herself for later.

'You're not going to tell me, are you,' he said with keen perception, and she shook her head slowly.

'No,' she managed, her voice cracking, and suddenly there was nothing she wanted more than to rest her head against his broad chest and to feel his strong arms supporting her.

Oh, God, she was so vulnerable at that moment that she would have accepted anything from him. Even pity!

His hands brushed her hair away from her face and tilted it up before she had time to blink away her tears. His features became blurred as he lowered his head to hers, and a faint gasp of surprise escaped her when she felt his lips brushing the tears from her eyes. Sean's breath was warm against her cheek, and there was the faint smell of the cheroots he always smoked before his mouth shifted over hers. Her lips parted beneath his in response, and a slow quivering warmth erupted inside her. His mouth moved against hers, savouring, exploring, and with a smothered little cry deep down in her throat she leaned weakly against him and slid her hands around his waist and up across his broad back to cling to his shoulders.

The world stopped spinning on its axis, and time was measured in heartbeats as their kiss deepened with a passion that seemed to consume them both in its flames. Sarika's body was arched against Sean's, the muscled hardness of his thighs against her own, and her breasts hurting against his chest. She was beyond caring when he held her a little away from him to slide her robe and nightie off her shoulders. She was conscious only of his dark, smouldering eyes devouring her as her body was revealed to him.

'God, Sarika, but you're beautiful!' he groaned, pulling her back into his arms, and desire instilled a certain roughness in his touch as he lowered his head to seek out the sensitive areas at the base of her throat and below her ear.

His lips were like a sensual fire against her skin, arousing and exciting hidden little nerves until she shivered with pleasure, and his arms tightened about her, curving her soft, yielding body into his with an urgency that made her aware of a new tension in his hard, muscled frame. *He wanted her*. If there could never be anything else, then she could always remember that he wanted her at that moment as much as she wanted him, and a joyous sensation surged through her veins that left her weak with the force of it as he lifted her in his arms and carried her towards the bed.

The sheets were cool and soft beneath her, but Sean's body was warm and hard above her as he sought her mouth with his and kissed her deeply and almost violently. Crazy with a burning desire to touch him as he was touching her, she tugged his sweat-shirt out of his belt, and he raised himself to peel it off and throw it aside. She caressed his hair-roughened chest, his wide shoulders, his back, her palms savouring the slight dampness of his skin stretched so tautly across the hardened muscles, and he lowered himself on to her with a shudder to bury his face against her throat. His hands cupped her small, firm breasts, his thumbs caressing the hardened nipples, and his touch sent a warm surge of desire rippling through her.

'Oh, Sean!' she gasped as his mouth trailed down to her breast to continue the arousal his fingers had started, and her desire was almost a pain when he raised himself slightly to devour her once again with his eyes.

A low animal-sounding growl passed his lips. 'My God, honey, I want you!'

Her drugged mind issued a warning, but Sean had

lowered his head, and the tip of his tongue was trailing lazy, sensual circles around her swollen nipple. Her breath came jerkily over her parted lips at the pleasure he was arousing, and that aching warmth spread like fire into the lower half of her taut body when he took the swollen peak into his warm, moist mouth.

'Oh, God!' she moaned, desire shuddering through her, but there was no help from above as her desire mounted with each caress of that sensual mouth on her responsive flesh.

He was arousing her to the point of pain, and her treacherous body was responding to the touch of his fingers as he trailed them across her smooth thigh, her flat stomach, and finally the most intimate part of her body. Her hands gripped his shoulders in a somewhat spasmodic action as a stab of intense pleasure shot through her. She wanted to push him away when he parted her legs with his thigh, and yet she could not, but her instincts warned against the outcome if she continued to allow such intimacies.

I have to stop him! The thought screamed through her mind, and sanity was like an icy bath in England's winter.

'Sean!' she cried his name, her hands pushing at his heavy body. 'Sean, I've never——'

'Never what?' he demanded, his eyes narrowed and black with desire, and something in the way she looked at him must have given him the answer. 'My God, you're a virgin!'

There was a hint of disgust in his incredulous voice, and Sarika cringed beneath his gaze, her face paling as he rolled away from her and sat on the edge of the bed with his head in his hands. His breathing was as laboured as her own, and she lay there staring at him with eyes that were dark with pain and the stormy emotions he had aroused.

'Sean, I'm sorry,' she whispered huskily, her body aching for the fulfilment it was denied, and blaming herself for what had occurred. She reached out tentatively to touch his arm, but he jerked it away as if her touch repelled him.

'For God's sake, why didn't you tell me!' His voice grated harshly against raw nerves, and his eyes blazed down into hers accusingly. 'Dammit, Sarika, if there's something I always swore never to do then it's to get involved with a virgin!'

Sarika's icy body shivered uncontrollably when he got up, pulled on his sweat-shirt, and strode out of her room. She sat up slowly, staring at the door he had slammed behind him, and she hid her quivering mouth behind her fingers as hot, stinging tears filled her eyes and rolled down her pale cheeks. She tasted the salt of them in her mouth, and wished suddenly that she was dead. Sean was a man accustomed to taking his women to bed, and she knew now exactly what he thought of her. He had wanted her simply to add her name to the long list of women who had passed through his hands, while she had wanted him out of a desperate need born of love. She had been wrong to encourage him, and she blamed herself entirely, but how it had hurt to hear the disgust in his voice.

If Sarika could have wished herself at the far ends of the earth during the next few days, then she would have done so. Sean had been in a foul and explosive mood since the Sunday night after he had stormed out of her room, and everyone in the office, including Sarika, felt as if they were treading on thin ice. Sarika especially suffered the brunt of his fury when he stormed into her office the Wednesday afternoon and slammed a file down on to her desk with a force that made her jump.

'Explain this to me!' he thundered at her.

She stared at the file, and she was reminded of the most unpleasant incident which had occurred during the week Sean had been away. 'It's the Lockwood file.'

'Baby, I'm not blind!' roared Sean, the veins standing out on his forehead, and his eyes darting flames of fury at her. 'What I want to know is why the contract was cancelled?'

'Mr Lockwood is an objectionable slob who wouldn't stop pawing me when we met for lunch to discuss the plans for the extension to his business premises,' she explained with a calmness she dredged from somewhere. 'When I finally succeeded in bringing the conversation round to the plans, he had the gall to tell me he never discussed business with women, so I tore up his contract, dumped it in his dessert, and told him to take his business elsewhere.'

'You did what?' Sean exploded, placing his hands on her desk and leaning towards her as if he wanted to demolish her with the black fury in his eyes. 'Do you know how much that contract was worth?'

'I know it was worth a small fortune,' she said coldly, 'and you don't have to shout, I'm not deaf.'

'God help me, I could——' His fingers groped in the air as if he was tempted to take her by the throat, then he lowered his hands and flicked the switch on her intercom system. 'Miranda, get me Lockwood on the line to Sarika's office, and it's urgent!' he snapped, flicking the switch back to its original position before Miranda could acknowledge his request.

'You're surely not going to crawl to him?' Sarika exclaimed incredulously.

'Business is business, lady, and if I have to crawl because of your damn stupidity, then I'll crawl.' The telephone rang loudly, and he snatched up the receiver. 'Yes? Put him on!' he barked into the instrument while his eyes on Sarika's white face continued their punishment. 'Lockwood?' he said a moment later. 'O'Connor here from Apex.'

What followed was a rather one-sided conversation with Sean listening more often than participating. His dark brows were drawn together in a frown, and when he replaced the receiver he studied Sarika through narrowed eyes for several harrowing seconds.

'What did he say?' she asked when she could no longer bear the tension of waiting and wondering.

'He said he liked your style, and he's coming in tomorrow so that you can draw up a new contract with a couple of additions.' Her obvious surprise brought a strangely twisted smile to his otherwise stern mouth. 'Do you know something, Sarika? I kinda like your style too.'

He strode out of her office and left her sitting there with the feeling that she was dangling somewhere between incredulity and anger, but there was also the niggling suspicion that Sean had not referred entirely to the way she had handled Mr Lockwood. Her cheeks went hot as humiliating memories crowded her mind, but she brushed them aside instantly and concentrated on her work.

She did not see Sean again to find out whether his mood had altered at all, neither did she see him when she left the office shortly after five that evening. It took some time to get out of the city and on to the road to Malabar Hills, but when she was approaching the house she noticed Sean's Land Rover coming up swiftly behind her. Sarika garaged her car, but he left the Land Rover in the driveway, and she was surprised to see him waiting for her when she walked round the house to the main entrance.

'I owe you an apology for slamming you this afternoon, and I think you deserve to be complimented,' he said, taking her arm as they mounted the steps to the front door, and he was smiling that odd, twisted smile again. 'I threw you in at the deep end last week, and you managed pretty well.'

'Except for the Lockwood contract which I almost lost,' she added with a touch of cynicism.'

'Except for the Lockwood contract,' Sean agreed mockingly, 'but that was quite understandable.'

Sarika felt a little warmth intrude on the coldness which had invaded her heart a few nights ago, but there was still a hint of cynicism in her smile when she glanced up at him. 'I'm glad you see it that way.'

'Let's have a drink before we go up and change for dinner,' Sean suggested when they entered the house, but Ayah came bustling towards them before Sarika could reply.

'You have a visitor, Sean,' announced Ayah with a strange tightness about her mouth instead of her usual welcoming smile, and she turned to lead the way into the living-room.

A woman of about Sean's age rose from the chair beside the tall brass ewer. Her auburn hair was cut and styled in a sleek cap about her classic features, and her pale blue, wide-sleeved dress was of a soft, clinging material that emphasised her perfectly proportioned body. She was, Sarika decided, one of the most beautiful women she had ever seen.

'Elvira!' Sean exclaimed throatily. 'Elvira Duncan!'

'Sean darling!' Crimson lips parted in a smile to display evenly spaced pearly teeth as she floated into Sean's arms and kissed him with an easy familiarity that suggested past intimacies, and the thought stabbed at Sarika. 'Surprised to see me?'

'Not entirely,' smiled Sean, holding the woman a little away from him to look down into the limpid grey eyes. 'You have always had a habit of arriving unexpectedly in the oddest places, and at the oddest times.'

Her smile deepened provocatively. 'Well, here I am again, darling, and I hope you're pleased to see me.'

'I'm always pleased to see you, Elvira,' Sean replied smoothly, 'but I'd like to know what you're doing here without your husband.'

'Jerry and I have been divorced for some months now, and I'm treating myself to a cruise around the world. The ship docked at noon today, and after a sightseeing trip around the city I came straight here.' Diamonds glittered about Elvira Duncan's throat and on her slender fingers as she raised her hand to caress Sean's rugged cheek with that familiarity which sent yet another stab of jealousy through Sarika. 'I wanted to see your face when you walked in this evening, so I told your maid here not to let you know I had arrived.'

Sarika's back stiffened at Elvira's reference to Ayah as the maid, and she glanced swiftly at Ayah's tight features, but it was Sean who rectified the matter.

'Ayah is the housekeeper, and she's been part of Sarika's family for many years.' He disengaged himself from Elvira Duncan and his fingers closed lightly about Sarika's arm as he drew her closer. 'Let me introduce you, Elvira. This is Sarika Maynesfield.'

The grey eyes that met Sarika's had lost their warmth to become cold and calculating, and Sarika knew instinctively that this woman was her enemy.

'So you're Sarika.' The crimson lips smiled, but the eyes remained cold. 'When the maid ... er ... housekeeper mentioned your name I had visions of Sean living with someone older and more mature, and knowing his taste in woman I'm surprised to see he's stooped to cradle-snatching.'

Sarika did not need to be reminded of Sean's preferences where women were concerned, but Elvira's insinuation that Sarika was sharing Sean's bed was like a declaration of war. Elvira had launched the first attack, but Sarika parried it with a cool smile.

'I think a youthful partner adds spice to a relationship to make it last much longer, whereas with a woman of your age, Mrs Duncan, a relationship could peter out and become staid much sooner.'

Sean appeared to find the situation as well as Sarika's statement amusing, but the atmosphere between Sarika and Elvira Duncan was explosive as they stood assessing each other for a second bout.

'Are you staying to dinner, Mrs Duncan?' Ayah intruded tactfully, easing the situation a fraction.

'If I'm invited.' Elvira turned from Sarika to smile up at Sean provocatively, and the hand she placed on his arm was possessive. 'Am I, darling?'

'Naturally you're invited,' Sean agreed, escorting Elvira to the chair she had vacated on their arrival. 'We haven't seen each other for years, and we have a lot to catch up on.'

Sarika's fingers tightened spasmodically on the handle of her briefcase. 'If you'll excuse me, I'd like to go up and change.'

'Aren't you joining us for a drink, Sarika?' asked Sean, turning to face her with a sardonic lift to his eyebrow while Elvira's hand still rested in his.

'Not this time,' she declined, forcing a smile to her stiff lips. 'Since you have so much to catch up on I know I'd simply be in the way.'

Sarika followed Ayah from the living-room, and the smile on her lips faded to leave her features tense and drawn as she hurried up the stairs to her room. Elvira Duncan's tinkling laughter drifted up the stairs, and Sarika closed her bedroom door firmly to shut out the sound.

Her thoughts and emotions were in a turmoil when she ran her bath water and stripped off her clothes. Sean had once said that he had known many beautiful women, and Elvira Duncan was certainly one of them. She also wasn't a virgin! Sarika winced visibly. Why did she have to torture herself like this? Her thoughts returned to the woman downstairs in the living-room with Sean. Elvira Duncan's manner had clearly indicated that they had once been lovers, and now that she was free of her husband she was obviously hoping to pick up their relationship where they had left off.

Sarika groaned inwardly, and lowered her tense body into the hot, scented water. It was not very difficult for Sarika to imagine Elvira Duncan's beautiful body caught up in a passionate embrace with Sean, and the mere thought of it sent a searing stab of jealousy through Sarika.

'Oh, God!' she breathed in an anguished voice. 'Why do I have to feel this way about a man who doesn't want me?'

She tried desperately to relax, but when she stepped out of the bath half an hour later she was still as tense as she had been before. She had succeeded, though, in controlling her thoughts, and she dressed with considerable care that evening for dinner.

The dress she chose was her favourite, with off-the-shoulder gypsy sleeves reaching down to her slender wrists, and a close-fitting bodice that accentuated her small breasts and narrow waist. The skirt flared out to below her knees, and the soft, white material made her smooth skin seem more tanned than it actually was. She fastened a gold chain about her throat which had been a gift from her parents on her eighteenth birthday, and when she stepped back from the dressing table to study herself in the full-length mirror she looked calm and composed despite the fact that her insides felt as if they had been twisted into a million knots. She had left her hair free of the confining knot she preferred when she went to the office, and it hung in a heavy, silken mass down to below her shoulders. Her make-up was applied with a subtleness that enhanced the beauty of her eyes, and her soft pink lipstick added the required touch to her full, sensitive mouth.

Sarika felt satisfied with herself when she left her room and went downstairs, but she was not looking forward to Elvira Duncan's company at the dinner table. The heels of her white high-heeled sandals clicked loudly on the marble floor as she crossed the hall, and the sound of that lilting voice in the living-room made Sarika square her shoulders before she went in.

Sean had somehow had sufficient time to shower and change into brown corded pants and a cream shirt, and as always, the impact he made on Sarika had the power to quicken her pulse rate. He poured a sherry for Sarika, and she was aware of his dark glance lingering like fire on her bare shoulders and small breasts when he handed her her glass. He had made her feel naked, as if she was trying to tempt him with her body, and she regretted suddenly that she had chosen to wear that particular dress. Sean turned away from her to give his attention to Elvira, but instead of feeling relieved,

Sarika felt oddly as if she had been shut out. Elvira's glance met Sarika's a moment later, and the look in those cold grey eyes said clearly, 'He's mine! I want him! And I intend to have him!'

Sarika had no defence against that. Sean would never belong entirely to any woman, least of all to someone like herself, and she withdrew quietly behind that mental flag of defeat.

Ayah came in a moment later to announce that dinner would be served, but she did not join them at the dinner table that evening. Sean frowned his displeasure at her absence, but Elvira captured his attention, and he left the matter there.

Sarika had no appetite for the tastefully prepared food, and every mouthful seemed to lodge uncomfortably in her throat before she succeeded in swallowing it down. Elvira, however, seemed to sparkle at the dinner table, and her lilting voice and witty remarks brought a smile to Sean's lips which Sarika had never seen before. It softened his rugged features until she could almost call him handsome, and a pain lodged somewhere in her chest at the knowledge that Elvira Duncan had the ability to make him look like that.

'I've persuaded Elvira to stay over a few days,' Sean told Sarika when they lingered at the table over coffee, and Sarika sat there feeling as if he had dropped a live bomb in her lap. 'She can always take a flight from here to join the cruise again at a different port of call.'

There was a hint of triumph in Elvira's smile as she directed her gaze at Sarika. 'I hope you don't mind?'

'As if I have the right to mind!' Sarika thought dismally, but her voice was cool and polite when she said: 'Not at all.'

Elvira turned her attention back to Sean. 'We'll have to collect some of my things off the ship.'

'We can do that later this evening,' suggested Sean, helping himself to a second cup of coffee.

'Oh, it's so wonderful to see you again, Sean.'

Elvira's American accent was suddenly very pronounced, and Sarika had difficulty in tearing her glance away from that slender, possessive hand caressing Sean's tanned forearm when Elvira turned to speak to her. 'We've known each other for many years, and there was a time when I believed we might get married, but Sean has an aversion to marriage which is unshakeable. We argued, and to spite him I married Jerry Duncan instead.' She turned her sleek head to gaze at Sean, and the look that passed between them excluded Sarika. 'It was a foolish thing to do, but I don't intend to make the same mistake again, darling.'

Sarika felt her insides quiver and tighten up into one aching knot. Elvira Duncan was out to get Sean. Since marriage seemed to be out, she would get him into her bed, and, judging by the smile that creased Sean's rugged features, Elvira's task was not going to be a difficult one.

The telephone rang in the hall, jarring Sarika's nerves, and she rose instantly from her chair. 'I'll take it.'

It was a relief to get out of the dining-room and away from Elvira Duncan's scintillating presence. It was a relief also not to see the way Sean seemed incapable of taking his eyes off the woman, and there was an unaccustomed brittleness in her voice when she lifted the receiver to her ear. 'Sarika Maynesfield speaking.'

'Sarika, this is Melissa,' a bright, youthful voice announced. 'Craig and I are going to venture out in Daddy's yacht this coming Saturday. We're bringing a friend of Craig's along, and I was hoping you would come with us to make a fourth. We've got the yacht for the whole day, so please say you'll come?'

'I'm not sure, Melissa, I——' The memory of how her parents had died was still too fresh in Sarika's mind, and she could not decide what to do. 'Could I let you know later?'

'I'll call you again on Friday.' There was a brief silence before Melissa added: 'Please, Sarika, I really do wish you'd come. We haven't seen you for simply ages, and it would be like old times.'

Sarika did not commit herself, but she promised to give it some thought before Melissa telephoned again, and they ended the conversation a few seconds later.

'Who was that?'

Sarika spun round nervously to find Sean standing no more than a pace away from her, and she avoided his probing glance by staring almost fixedly at the small medallion nestling among the dark chest hair where he had left his shirt unbuttoned.

'That was Melissa Armstrong,' she told him in a stilted voice. 'She's invited me to accompany Craig and herself and a friend on a day trip in her father's yacht this coming Saturday.'

There was an ominous silence before he asked: 'Are you going?'

'I haven't decided yet.'

'How experienced are they?'

'Craig and Melissa are both fairly experienced, but I'm not sure about the friend Craig is bringing along.'

'I wouldn't go if I were you.'

Sarika's head shot up defiantly, and resentment sparkled in her eyes when they met his. 'I'm perfectly capable of making my own decisions, thank you.'

'Don't do anything idiotic, Sarika,' he warned, and, turning on his heel, he strode back to the dining-room where Elvira was waiting for him.

Sarika did not follow him. She turned instead and went up to her room. If Elvira Duncan was going to be a guest in this house, then she wanted to see as little of her as possible.

It was a hot, balmy night, and Sarika opened her windows wider to let in more air when she went to bed. She did not sleep very well that night for various other reasons, and neither did she get much sleep during the days that followed.

Sean did not come to the office during Elvira's visit. They met at the breakfast table each morning, Sarika forced herself to be polite to both Sean and Elvira, then they did not see each other again until breakfast the following day. She knew that Sean and Elvira left the house shortly after she had left for the office, and she knew also that they did not return until late at night. What they did, and where they went, she did not know, neither did she want to, but her mind conjured up visions of shared intimacies that seemed to want to drive her to the point of insanity. If they had been lovers before, her cruel mind pointed out, then they could be lovers again, and she felt the savage thrust of anguish and jealousy like a dagger piercing her breast.

She somehow managed to get through her work at the office, but she dreaded going home at night, despite the fact that Ayah tried to cheer her up by preparing her favourite dishes, and she was at her lowest ebb when Melissa telephoned on the Friday evening. She was incapable of thinking rationally. The only thought that pounded through her mind was the knowledge that she had to get out of that house while Elvira was still there as Sean's guest, and it was with this thought in mind that she answered Melissa's query.

'I'll come with you.'

'Good!' Melissa exclaimed over the telephone. 'Meet us at the yacht at seven-thirty tomorrow morning.'

CHAPTER TEN

SARIKA was awake an hour before the alarm went off the following morning. She got up, washed and dressed herself in white shorts and a sleeveless yellow knitted top, then she packed her bikini and suntan lotion into a small tog bag. She scribbled a short note to Ayah to let her know where she was going, but it was still too early to leave the house. She drew aside the curtains to stare out beyond the garden towards the city in the distance, and a slight frown appeared between her arched brows. The sky was overcast, predicting rain, but Sarika was in a foolishly optimistic mood. The weather would have cleared by the time she reached the harbour, and it was with this thought in mind that she left the house a half hour later.

The engine of the Mercedes sports purred like a kitten when she turned the key in the ignition, then she was speeding down the drive and away from the house. The streets were still free of traffic at that time of the morning, and it did not take her long to reach the harbour where Melissa and Craig awaited her. Craig's friend, Paul Tanner, arrived some minutes later, and of the three Sarika found him the most serious-minded and mature for his youthful age.

They took their things on board the gleaming white yacht, and only when Sarika felt it rolling beneath her did common sense prevail. She glanced up at the grey sky with the dark clouds looming in the distance, and logic warned that it would be unsafe to go out in the yacht that morning.

'I think we should postpone this trip for some other time when the weather looks more promising,' Sarika proffered her advice to Melissa and Craig. 'It looks like we're in for a storm.'

'I think I agree with you,' Paul added his opinion to that of Sarika's. 'Let's leave it for another time.'

'Oh, don't be silly, you two!' laughed Melissa carelessly. 'There are still a few weeks left to enjoy ourselves before the monsoon period begins, so stop being so pessimistic, and let's get going.'

The *Sea Nymph* heaved and sagged beneath Sarika, and her logical mind warned again that they were making a grave mistake, but the thought of returning home made her cast aside her wariness. She did not want to spend the day alone at home with Ayah, neither did she fancy accompanying Sean and Elvira to wherever they might care to go. Only one choice remained, and that was to go with Melissa, Craig, and the dubious-looking Paul.

The *Sea Nymph* was a large, motor-driven yacht with two cabins and a spacious deck on which to suntan, but Sarika did not imagine she would be doing much sunbathing in this weather. She felt the vibration of the engines beneath her, then they were leaving the harbour and heading out towards the sea.

It was *all hands on deck* for a time, with Craig at the helm, and the rest of them rushing around to carry out his instructions. They were some miles out to sea when the weather cleared slightly, and Craig cut the engines so that they could lounge about on the deck and help themselves to something to eat and drink. Paul was pleasant and undemanding company, and Sarika eventually slipped into a dreamless sleep from which she was awakened with a start some time later with the feeling that she was being jolted about. She was not alone on the deck. Paul stood gripping the low rail close to her and staring out across a sea which had become rough and choppy while she had slept.

A film of mist had sprung up from nowhere, and it was beginning to surround them when Sarika joined Paul at the rail. 'I know it's too late to say this now, but we definitely shouldn't have come out in the yacht today, and I wish Craig and Melissa had listened to us,' he said grimly.

Sarika cast a searching glance across the deck. 'Where are Melissa and Craig?'

'They went below a few minutes ago to——' A giant wave rose unexpectedly to crash against the side of the *Sea Nymph.* It soaked them to the skin and there was water everywhere as it sent them sprawling across the deck. 'Get below,' Paul shouted to Sarika, 'and send Craig up to help me at the helm!'

Stay calm, Sarika! Stay calm! she warned herself as she crawled across the heaving, rocking deck, and she somehow managed to get below without injuring herself.

'Paul needs your help at the helm,' she told Craig when he burst out of one of the cabins before she could knock. 'Where's Melissa?'

'She's in there.' He pointed with his thumb over his shoulder to the cabin from which he had just emerged. 'I suggest you stay with her while Paul and I sort out this problem.'

He squeezed past Sarika in the narrow passage and clambered up the steps on to the deck, while Sarika stood there being jolted about like a limp doll. The yacht rolled violently again, and Sarika was thrown forward so that she lunged into the cabin to find Melissa lying curled into a ball on one of the bunks. She thought at first that Melissa was ill, but when she looked into those wide green eyes she saw naked terror.

'For God's sake, Melissa!' Sarika rebuked her angrily. 'You're the one who got us into this mess, and it's up to you to help get us out of it!'

'I'm scared!' wailed Melissa, her face almost as white as the pillow beneath her head.

'I'm just as scared,' Sarika shouted out her confession, 'but getting into a panic isn't going to help!'

Melissa refused to budge and, losing patience with her, Sarika left the cabin and climbed up on to the deck to face the elements.

The sky had become dark and ominous, and the sea was getting rougher by the second, but somehow she managed to reach Craig and Paul in the control cabin where they clung to the helm with every ounce of strength they possessed. The engines were throbbing beneath her feet, but Sarika knew they would never reach Bombay safely in this weather despite the *Sea Nymph*'s powerful engines.

The storm broke loose in all its fury a few minutes later, and the yacht was bounced about like a cork. The bow rose and fell, sending a spray of frothy water across the deck while the turbulent sea rocked them from port to starboard at a nauseating pace. Drenched and shivering, Sarika stood clutching at a rail for support in the tiny control cabin.

'There's a small island not far from here, but it's surrounded by a coral reef,' Craig shouted above the noise of the storm. 'There's a break in the reef to the north side of the island. If we can make it through that opening, then we'll be safe on the island until the storm has passed.'

'You're crazy!' shouted Paul. 'We'll never make it!'

'We've got to try!' Craig shouted back at him, the muscles in their arms and shoulders bulging as they clung to the helm while the sea lifted them repeatedly and flung them back into the water.

Sarika could not stand there doing nothing while Craig and Paul fought to control the yacht and keep it on course through a current which seemed determined to take them elsewhere. Someone had to make the necessary preparations in case of an emergency, and common sense warned that the safest place in a disaster would be on the deck.

She went down below once again, clinging to the rails on either side of her wherever she could for fear of losing her footing and being flung overboard. Melissa was still in her cabin, and she was lying on her bunk with her clenched fist in her mouth. Sarika's own fear made her want to scream abuse at her friend, but she knew this was not going to help. She had to remain calm, and she had to motivate Melissa into giving them assistance.

'Listen to me, Melissa,' she said as calmly as she could. 'You can't lie here like this while there's work to be done. I need your help; we all need your help, and you must pull yourself together.'

'We're going to die! Oh, God, we're going to die!' Melissa screamed hysterically. 'I should have listened to you, and we should have stayed at home, but instead we're out here in this stinking weather and we're all going to die!'

Sarika stood there clutching at the top bunk for support and dripping sea water on the carpeted floor. She was staring at the hysterical girl lying on the lower bunk, but her mind was elsewhere at that moment. She was thinking about her parents and how they had died, and fear almost choked off her breath at the thought that she was going to die in a similar manner, but Melissa's hysterical sobbing brought her swiftly back to reality. She had to do something about Melissa, and she had to do it quickly. Her hand shot out, and she slapped the girl hard across the cheek.

'No one is going to die, do you hear me!' she shouted as she dragged a miraculously silent Melissa to her feet. 'I won't let it happen, and you're going to help me!'

Melissa was all at once like a subdued child ready to take instructions from a superior. 'What do you want me to do?'

'Show me where the lifejackets are kept, and let's get on deck so we can be on hand if our help is needed in the control cabin.'

Brushing her wispy blonde hair out of her eyes, Melissa led the way out of the cabin to a small cupboard below the steps that led up on to the deck. She slid open the door and produced four bright orange lifejackets. They were helping each other don their jackets when Sarika noticed a small first aid kit on a shelf against the wall. Realising that they might need it if one of them should be injured, she took it off the shelf and pushed it into the zip-up pocket of the lifejacket before they went up the steps to join Craig and Paul.

The driving rain and the spray of sea water washing over the deck had drenched both the girls by the time they stumbled into the control cabin, and Sarika's teeth were beginning to chatter with the cold. The two men looked as nauseous as Sarika was beginning to feel when she helped them into the lifejackets, but it was a difficult task to accomplish while the men had to put all their weight to the helm of their wildly rocking yacht.

'I've radioed through an S.O.S., but I don't know whether anyone picked it up,' Paul shouted the information to Sarika.

She was about to suggest that he show her how to use the radio so that she could repeat the request for assistance, but the *Sea Nymph* lurched violently in the storm-tossed sea, and sent her stumbling towards the opposite side of the tiny cabin where Melissa had crouched some minutes ago with a new look of terror in her eyes.

How long could they still survive in this weather? Sarika was fast becoming frantic with fear as the yacht creaked and groaned in protest beneath her. Would this nightmare ever end?

'The island should be just up ahead of us,' Craig proffered the information as if he had read Sarika's thoughts. 'If we can get round it to the north side, then our troubles are over.'

Sarika shivered and clung to that fragile hope. On the floor beside her Melissa sat white-faced but silent, and Sarika momentarily brushed her own fears aside to comfort her friend.

'We have a chance to land safely on the island,' she said, gripping Melissa's hand briefly. 'Hang on to that thought, Melissa.'

It was all very well telling Melissa what to do, but Sarika was not coping so very well with her own fears.

She thought of her parents, and wondered why fate had decided that her life should end in a similar way. Sean's rugged features leapt into her mind, and she longed for the strength of his arms about her.

'Oh, Sean, Sean!' her heart wept. 'If only you could have loved me too!'

An eternity seemed to pass before the men shouted that the island was in sight through the mist. Sarika and Melissa were instantly on their feet, clutching at the railings as they watched the two men battle at the helm to keep the yacht off the reef as they steered it in a north-westerly direction towards the opening in the barrier Craig had spoken of. Rocks suddenly jutted out of the sea, and Sarika stood with her heart beating in her mouth for fear that they might hit one of them.

The wind was a howling force behind the rain, and the sea was like a wild horse trying to fling the yacht off its back. The bow lifted towards a rock that appeared suddenly in front of it, but the yacht was flung aside the next instant to pass it safely.

'Damn these rocks!' shouted Paul. 'We came in too close to the island, and we're never going to make it!'

Those words had barely been spoken when they felt the shuddering impact of the yacht's hull on rocks which had been hidden beneath the swirling surface of the sea. The engines cut out at once, and the jarring sound of splintering wood was in Sarika's ears as she was flung against the rail on impact. An excruciating stab of pain in her side made her lose her grip on the rail, and she fell to the floor of the control cabin with Paul and Craig almost on top of her. A cry of terror rose in her throat, but she bit it back when Melissa's piercing scream rang out above the noise of the storm. Again and again Melissa screamed until Sarika managed to get on to her hands and knees to crawl towards the hysterical girl.

'Shut up, Melissa, this is no time for hysterics!' she spoke sharply to the girl. 'We're all in this together, and we have to stay together and work together if we're going to come out of this alive.'

'We must inflate the raft,' instructed Craig when they heard the ominous sound of water gurgling and gushing into the yacht.

Paul leapt into action, and Craig followed with Sarika and a white-faced Melissa hard on his heels, but they never succeeded in inflating the dinghy. The yacht lurched once more as a giant wave lifted it beyond the rocks and on to the reef. The hull was completely shattered on impact, and Sarika felt the blood drain away from her face to leave her as deathly white as her three companions. She knew what this meant. The *Sea Nymph* was sinking, they all knew it, but Melissa perhaps more than the rest of them. She had gone beyond mere hysteria, and they watched with stupefied eyes as Melissa slid on to the deck in a dead faint.

'We'll have to swim for it, and there's no time to waste!' Sarika yelled when the three of them had failed to revive Melissa. 'The yacht isn't going to remain stable for long, and if we stay here a moment longer we're going to be thrown against the rocks.'

The two men stared helplessly at Melissa's lifeless body, and Sarika knew they were just as frightened as she was. Melissa was a burden at that moment; a burden which could cost them their lives, but their consciences would not let them go and leave her. The yacht was still reasonably stable, but no one knew for how long. There was no time to lose, and they were wasting precious seconds. It was then that Sarika took charge. She ordered Criag into the raging, bucking sea and, with Paul's help, Sarika lowered the unconscious Melissa into Craig's waiting hands. Paul followed next, and the yacht was sinking swiftly when Sarika finally jumped into the freezing water.

What followed was a nightmare Sarika knew she would never forget if she survived this ordeal. Between the three of them they managed to battle through the water. The lifejackets kept them afloat, but they were cumbersome to swim in, and they were at their wits' end when Melissa came to her senses, only to panic and scream hysterically. She thrashed about wildly, endangering all their lives, and this time it was Paul's fist that shot out to deliver a blow to Melissa's jaw that rendered her unconscious once more.

Sarika was aware of the pain in her side, and it felt as if every muscle was being strained to its limit as they fought to reach an island which seemed to be drifting farther away from them in the swirling mist. They had heard a terrible crashing sound behind them, but none of them looked back. It was as if they were all afraid to see nothing but the black sea and the mist where the *Sea Nymph* should have been.

They managed to stay together as they struggled towards the island with their heavy burden between them, and, after what seemed like hours, they were spat out into shallower water. They staggered out of the icy ocean with Melissa, and they had to drag her on to the beach where they collapsed on the wet sand. Panting and exhausted beyond their endurance, they lay stretched out on the beach while the rain beat down on them. It was a miracle they were alive, and they all knew it!

'We made it! Oh, God, we made it!' moaned Sarika, then reaction set in. She was trembling all over, and she curled her fingers into the sand to make sure she was not dreaming.

Melissa coughed and started to cry, and Sarika struggled instantly to her knees to raise her friend up into a sitting position. She could not keep her own tears of relief back when she looked into Melissa's eyes, and the two girls clung to each other, crying and laughing a little hysterically.

Paul and Craig recovered swiftly and instructed them to stay on the beach while they went in search of shelter from the storm. The two girls sat huddled together, trying to keep each other warm. Neither of them spoke while they waited, and it seemed as if yet another eternity had passed before the men returned with the news that they had found a place which would give them protection from the rain.

They staggered up the beach, and fought their way through the undergrowth beneath the trees until they came to a natural clearing. What the men had found was a cave. It was not high enough to stand up in, but it was big enough to accommodate all four of them. Stooping down, they entered it and lowered themselves on to the dry sand beneath them. They took off their lifejackets and sat in silence for some time, each busy with their own thoughts until they were capable of assessing the situation. Paul had sustained no injuries, Melissa's jaw felt a bit stiff and bruised after the vicious blow Paul had given her, but Craig had nicked his foot on the coral, and Sarika's side was beginning to throb painfully. Sarika had the first aid kit to attend to their injuries, but they were without food and drinking water, and God only knew how long they would have to stay on that island before they were found.

Sarika attended to Craig's foot, but there was nothing she could do about the ugly bruise darkening the skin against her right side. She was cold and she was shivering, and they had nothing with which to light a fire even if they could find a few dry twigs. They sat huddled together, trying to stay warm while the storm continued to rage outside. Conversation was sadly lacking, but when they did speak it was to thank God they were still alive.

The storm had passed by five-thirty that afternoon, but the nightmare had not ended. Craig's foot had become inflamed, and his temperature was rising steadily and dangerously. Melissa sat curled up in a tight ball, saying nothing and doing nothing, and that left Sarika and Paul to cope with the task of looking after Craig.

'I'm hungry,' Melissa complained as the sky darkened and the long night lay ahead of them.

'We're all hungry!' Sarika snapped at her. 'There's

nothing we can do about it, so there's no sense in complaining.'

Melissa curled up on the sand like a petulant child, and she promptly went to sleep. Sarika stared at her incredulously, but Craig groaned in pain, and she turned at once to attend to him.

During the night Sarika kept him cool with sea water which Paul fetched in the shallow lid which they had broken off the first aid kit. By midnight Sarika was beginning to feel equally feverish. Her body was aching, and it seemed an effort to move about.

'Sarika?' Paul's hand touched her shoulder. 'I'll stay up with Craig while you get some sleep.'

Sarika did not argue. She crawled across to where she knew Melissa was lying sleeping, and she curled herself up on the sand with a weariness in her mind and her body. She went to sleep instantly, but in her dreams she was on the yacht, and it was crumbling beneath her. Death reached out to her from the depths of the dark sea, but Sean was calling her to safety, and she hovered somewhere in between, incapable of deciding. The dream went on and on until the fingers of death licked at her skin, and she awoke abruptly to discover that it was morning. Paul was crouching beside her, his eyes heavy with lack of sleep, and somehow Sarika managed to rouse herself sufficiently to move over to Craig while Paul collapsed on the sand and slept.

Craig's fever had not broken, and Sarika was equally feverish as she sat there next to him. She bathed his fiery forehead, but her mind was still occupied with her dream. If she had to die, then she would have been happy doing so in Sean's arms. He did not care for her, but somehow that did not seem to matter. He would be there, and that was all she would need.

Her heart cried out her love for him, but her lips remained silent as she continued to bathe Craig's forehead like an automaton. Her body was aching, her head was throbbing, and her vision was becoming blurred. When oblivion threatened to claim her she tried to call Paul, but she could not get a sound past her burning throat. She had no idea how much time had passed before a mist finally enveloped her mind, and she lowered her shivering, aching body on to the sand. The heat of Craig's body warmed her, but her feverish mind told her it was Sean lying there next to her, and she felt comforted and protected against that terrible cold which had penetrated into her bones. She nestled closer, her arm sliding across his chest, and the next instant she felt herself sliding into a pit of darkness.

Sarika awakened several hours later to the sensation that she was burning up inside, and her chest was so tight that she could scarcely breathe. She was aware of being dragged out into the blinding sunlight, then someone's head came between her and the sun, and she was looking up into Sean's grim, unshaven face. The fury in his eyes seemed to add to the fire in her body when he lifted her in his arms and carried her away from the cave, but in her delirium there was a brief moment of clarity. It was Craig who was lying so gravely ill in the cave, not Sean, and concern made her struggle feebly against the pressure of the hard arms holding her.

'No, no!' she croaked hoarsely. 'I can't leave Craig! He needs me! I must——'

'Shut up and be still!' that harsh, familiar voice instructed, and she mercifully sank into a state of semi-consciousness.

She was aware of being placed on a stretcher and lifted into a helicopter. She was aware also of a second stretcher being lifted into the helicopter. She could hear Paul and Melissa talking almost simultaneously, but most of all she was aware of Sean's voice issuing harsh commands, and the blazing fury in his dark eyes whenever she surfaced sufficiently to find him leaning over her.

If one could feel safe, but also threatened, then that was exactly how Sarika felt when they were being flown back to Bombay and safety.

* * *

It was not until the early hours of the Monday morning that Sarika emerged from her state of feverish delirium to find Sean slumped in a chair beside her bed.

'Where am I?' she asked weakly, her eyes taking in the high white walls surrounding her.

'You're in hospital,' that deep, gravelly voice informed her, and she turned her head again to look at him. 'You've got pneumonia, and you're lucky you didn't crack a rib.'

His eyes were bloodshot and heavy-lidded as if he had not slept for days, and his rugged features were grim and drawn. 'You look terrible,' she said candidly.

'You don't look so good yourself,' he smiled twistedly, his strong fingers gripping hers, and it was then that the memory of the terrible ordeal she had suffered suddenly flooded her mind.

'Craig?' she murmured, a hint of terror lurking in her eyes. 'How is he? Do you know?'

'He's recovering, and he'll be out of hospital in a day or two.' Sean's features hardened, and the smile left his eyes to leave them cold. 'The other two were lucky enough to escape with nothing more than a slight cold.'

The knowledge that everyone was safe acted like a sedative, and Sarika drifted into a dreamless sleep from which she did not awaken until several hours later, but this time it was to find Ayah sitting next to her bed.

'Sarika, *pyaari*, we have been nearly out of our minds with worry, but I thank God that you are safe,' wept Ayah, clasping Sarika's hand between hers.

'I'm sorry, Ayah,' Sarika murmured tiredly, then she cast a searching glance about her. 'Where's Sean?'

'I persuaded him at last to go home,' Ayah explained his absence, releasing Sarika's hand to dab at her eyes with a lacy handkerchief. 'The poor man has not slept since we were notified of the distress signal coming from the *Sea Nymph*. The most terrible thing was that we could do nothing in the storm, and then it was too dark to start a search before morning.' Ayah's eyes clouded as she shook her head. 'I've never before seen a man so demented with concern.'

Demented? Sean *demented* with concern for her? *Impossible!* 'Where's Elvira Duncan?' Sarika asked.

'She left on Saturday morning.' Ayah's lips tightened with displeasure. 'Sean drove her to the airport after breakfast.'

How ironic, Sarika thought, suppressing the desire to laugh hysterically. It was because of Elvira Duncan that she had accepted Melissa's invitation, but it had all been so unnecessary.

Ayah did not stay long, but she left Sarika with something to think about. If Sean had been so demented with concern for her safety, then why had he been so angry when he had found her? A little spark of hope was lit inside her, but she doused it almost at once.

Melissa came to see her that evening, but the nurse would not let her closer than the doorway because of her cold.

'I'm relieved you're better,' said Melissa in a subdued, remorseful voice. 'Your Mr O'Connor was more than ordinarily annoyed, and he made it quite clear that he would blame me if anything happened to you.'

'It's over, Melissa, and we're all safe.' Sarika's mind cynically rejected Melissa's statement. 'That's what really matters, isn't it?'

'I suppose so,' Melissa nodded gravely. They talked a while longer, then she left to go and see Craig, and Sarika closed her eyes, glad to be alone again.

During the days that followed Sarika had brief visits from Craig as well as Paul. Michael had heard about the accident and came twice to see her. Ayah called in every day, but Sean never came again. *Why?* If he had been so concerned about her, and if he had been so annoyed with Melissa because of what had happened, then why could he not spare the time to come and see her? She wanted to question Ayah about it, but she was afraid of what she might hear, so the subject was never mentioned.

Sarika was allowed to go home the Saturday morning, and she sat in a chair studying herself in the hand mirror while she waited for Ayah. The nurses had washed her hair and it had regained some of its lustre, but her face was pale, and there were purple smudges like bruises beneath her eyes. Her hand went absently to her side. She had bruised herself badly, but it was now no more than a sensitive discoloration. She was lucky; they were all lucky to have got off so lightly!

The door to her ward was pushed open, and she looked up expecting to see Ayah, but instead it was Sean who walked into the ward with her overnight bag in his hand. His eyes were dark and shuttered when they met hers, and her pulse rate climbed rapidly when he dumped her bag on the bed and walked towards her. He was dressed exactly as he had been dressed that very first time she had seen him at the airport. The blue open-necked shirt still stretched too tightly across the width of his shoulders, and the white slacks still hugged his lean hips and accentuated the long muscular legs.

'How are you, Sarika?' he asked, his hands resting on his hips as he stood observing her intently.

What do you care? The words had hovered on her lips, but she bit them back to say casually, 'I'm fine.'

'You're looking much better,' he offered his opinion while he continued to study her with a strange glitter in his eyes.

'I feel much better, thank you,' she answered stiffly, her fingers nervously gripping the handle of the mirror when she sensed that his polite conversation was a cover for something explosive.

'I apologise for not seeing you during the week, but I had an urgent matter to attend to at the office in Australia, and I only arrived back late last night,' he explained the reason for his absence, and it was so far removed from what she had imagined that she wanted to burst into tears, but she managed to control herself.

'I understand,' she nodded with a little more warmth in her voice than when he had arrived.

Sarika met his probing glance, and for one crazy moment she thought she saw a flicker of something more than concern in his eyes, but it was gone the next instant. 'Get dressed so I can take you home,' he instructed in a clipped voice.

He walked out and left her feeling as if she had grasped at something only to find it gone, but the nurse came in a second later, and then there was no time to dwell on the matter.

Sean's silent, morose manner did not encourage conversation when he drove her home, and Sarika had the strangest feeling that yet another storm was brewing in which she would become involved. Ayah came hastily down the steps to welcome her when they arrived at the house, and her smiling embrace eased Sarika's nervousness. Sean came up beside Sarika when she was about to negotiate the steps, and she was lifted in his arms and carried into the house. She wanted to protest that she was capable of managing on her own, but the look on his stern face so close to hers forced her to remain silent as he carried her all the way up the stairs to her bedroom. Her heart bounced into her throat when he paused halfway across the room and tightened his arms about her. He turned his head, his lips inches from hers so that she could feel his warm, tobacco-scented breath against her mouth, and for one frantic moment she thought he was going to kiss her, but he turned his head away abruptly and continued across the room to lower her into the chair beside the window.

'You're to take it easy for the next few days,' he instructed when he stepped away from the chair. 'The doctor said you're not to do anything strenuous until you've fully regained your strength.'

Before Sarika could say anything he had strode out of the room to leave Ayah crooning over her.

'What can I bring you, Sarika?' Ayah wanted to

know, draping a light blanket over Sarika's legs. 'A cup of tea, perhaps?'

'That would be lovely,' Sarika agreed absently, and then she was alone with that terrible feeling that, for her, the storm was not yet over.

Four days passed during which she was pampered like a baby by an attentive, adoring Ayah. Sarika had been in bed on the Saturday evening when Sean came up to her room for a brief moment, she saw him twice the Sunday, and after that he came only in the evening when he returned home from the office. Their conversation was limited to enquiring after her health and remarking upon the steamy weather, but with each meeting Sarika's tension increased until she felt like a sitar string which was about to snap under pressure. She almost wished Sean would shout at her, or something equally drastic. *Anything*, she decided, would be preferable to those chilly courtesy calls he paid her.

CHAPTER ELEVEN

It was after nine on the Wednesday evening before Sean arrived home from the office. Sarika was reading a book in bed when she heard his Land Rover coming up the drive, and five minutes later there was a sharp tap on her door before it was pushed open. Sean walked in, the jacket of his dark grey, lightweight suit hooked on a finger over his shoulder, and his tie loosened so that he could unbutton his shirt collar. Black, smouldering eyes fastened on to hers when he closed the door and walked towards her bed, and she swallowed convulsively when she realised that the storm she had waited for was finally going to erupt. He flung his jacket across the foot of the bed, and his tie followed it. Ignoring the chair, he sat down beside her on the bed so that the springs sagged beneath his weight, and he undid two more buttons down the front of his white shirt.

Sarika stared at his deeply tanned, hair-roughened chest where that small silver medallion glinted in the bedside light. The desire to touch him was so incredibly strong at that moment that she had to close her book and curl her fingers tightly about it for fear she might succumb to her feelings only to be rejected.

'For God's sake, Sarika!' Sean's voice exploded into the tense silence. 'Why did you go out on that yacht when you knew there was a storm on the way?'

Sarika felt her insides twisting into a quivering knot. How could she tell him, 'I wanted to get away from you and Elvira, and I couldn't bear the thought of you being together'? She looked up to see impatience etched in every line of his rugged face, and gave him an answer which was only partly the truth. 'My judgment was clouded by my desire to get away from everything.'

'Do you have any idea what I went through during

those long hours before we found you the following day?' he snarled at her savagely, and she shrank mutely back against the pillows. 'No, I don't suppose you do! I suppose you think it didn't matter to me whether you were alive or dead!'

There was something in what he was saying that was reaching out to her, but she was too afraid to grasp it, and instead she contradicted his statement. 'I have a vague recollection that you weren't very pleased to see me. You were furious, if I remember correctly.'

'You're damn right I was furious!' he thundered at her. 'I'd spent hours thinking of everything I wanted to say to you if I was lucky enough to find you alive, and when I did find you you were locked in an embrace with what's-his-name as if he was the only thing that mattered to you.'

'If we were locked in an embrace, then it was simply because——'

'Go on!' he prompted harshly, but once again she shied away from the revealing truth.

'You have no right to expect an explanation from me while you leave the days and nights you spent with Elvira Duncan unexplained.' Oh, lord, what was she saying? she asked herself furiously, and Sean's eyes glittered strangely.

'Were you jealous?'

'Don't be ridiculous!' She brushed aside the truth.

'Elvira Duncan is an old friend. I took her to all the places I thought she'd like to see before I sent her packing the Saturday morning, and I don't imagine I'll see her again for another couple of years.' There was renewed fury in the eyes that held hers captive. 'Now you can tell me why I had to go out to that island to find you locked in an embrace with Craig Jenkins.'

'I was not embracing him, I was—oh, God!'

'Don't stop now, Sarika,' he goaded her savagely. 'Let me hear your version of what went on in that love-nest. Did you swop partners in the night? Is that why I found you clinging to Craig? Was he such a good lover, Sarika, that you were actually terrified I might leave him there to die?'

'Stop it! Stop it, do you hear me!' Her face was white, and her insides were shaking uncontrollably. 'It wasn't like that at all! Craig was burning up with fever, and Paul and I took turns caring for him. I was so ill eventually I didn't know what I was doing any more. I thought I was going to die, and all I could think of was *you.* I was cold and hot alternately because of the fever, and in my delirium I sought comfort from Craig's presence, but——' She broke off abruptly and buried her anguished face in her hands. 'God help me, Sean, but in my delirium I thought it was you!'

An awful silence followed her revealing explanation. She had been pressured into saying things she would never have said under normal circumstances, and she could not bear to look at Sean while she waited for him to lash her with his mockery and his contempt.

'Our relationship has been one big misunderstanding from the start, hasn't it?' She lowered her hands to stare at him in blank surprise. That was not what he was supposed to say. Where was his mockery, his disgust ... his rejection? He pushed his fingers uncharacteristically through his dark hair, and a new tension suddenly gripped her when his narrowed glance met hers. 'Sarika, listen to me! You've got to stop shutting me out because, God knows, I can't live with that! I want to know how interested you are in the Apex company. Do you intend to make a career of it to the exclusion of all else, or do you still have a secret desire to open up a boutique?'

'I don't know.' Her fingers tightened about the book in her lap to stop their trembling. 'I've been thinking these past few days that perhaps I ought to sell my shares in Apex, but I'm not so keen on the boutique either. Why do you ask?'

'I have a job to offer you which will involve a lot of travelling for the first year, but after that I intend to base myself more or less permanently in the United States while someone else does the travelling for me.'

Sarika was not quite sure what she had expected, but his words somehow filled her with an aching disappointment which she had difficulty in adjusting to. 'Are you offering me a job as your personal assistant?'

'What I'm offering you is a lifetime contract . . . a partnership.' His compelling glance held hers for several tense seconds, then he said: 'I want you to marry me.'

'No!' Shock cascaded through her like a charge of electricity to leave her rigid with rejection, and white as the pillows she was leaning against. 'You don't know what you're saying!'

There was an unfamiliar tremor in the hands that gripped her shoulders tightly and his features mirrored a torment she could not even begin to understand. 'I need you, and I don't want to have to live without you!'

A singing joy exploded inside her, but still she held back. 'Please, Sean, you're saying things you don't mean, and that's the cruellest thing you could ever do to me.'

'I love you, honey, and you've got to believe me that this is something I've never wanted to say to any woman before,' he said in a voice that was vibrant with emotion, and when she continued to stare at him in disbelief, he released her abruptly and pushed his fingers through his hair a second time as he got to his feet to pace the floor like a restless animal. 'Dammit, I've been so crazy with love for you that I actually wrote and told Maria about you, and she wrote back to tell me that she would never speak to me again if I let you slip through my fingers.'

'Maria?' she asked, holding her breath, for some extraordinary reason as her wary eyes followed him back and forth across the room.

'My sister,' he explained, ceasing his pacing to sit down beside her again. 'Her letter came from New York during my first trip to Australia.'

'Oh, God!' groaned Sarika, burying her face in her

hands as she recalled the anguish she had suffered because of that airmail letter from America.

'Trust me, Sarika,' Sean pleaded throatily, his fingers gentle as he took her hands away from her face. 'Please trust me?'

A bleak look entered her tawny eyes when they met his. 'The last time I—I trusted a man I——'

'You can't classify me in the same category as Gary Rowan,' Sean objected harshly, and she stared at him incredulously.

'You know about him?'

'Ayah told me.' He saw the blood surge into her cheeks and recede again to leave her pale, and his glance held hers relentlessly while he spoke. 'Ayah and I had a long talk during those hours while we waited to begin the search, and she told me a great many things about you that I know you would never have told me even if I'd threatened you with something drastic. I also got a well-deserved lecture from Ayah which was more like a dire warning. I had to sort out the problems between us soon, *or else*!' His wide shoulders sagged tiredly, but his fingers tightened about hers. 'I owe you an apology, Sarika, for some of the things I've said to you, but that was my way of digging for the truth.'

She felt a pulse jerking in her throat. 'Why was it so important to know the truth?'

'I wanted to know why I could never get through to you on a personal level, and I wanted to know what had hurt you so badly that you erected mental barriers not even I could penetrate at times. God, honey,' he groaned, 'I've wanted you from the first moment I saw you, and I almost had you that night you came back from Poona with Michael. I was so damn jealous when I saw you kissing him that I swore I'd make you pay, but I didn't bargain with the fact that you're a virgin and . . . oh, honey, it scared me when I realised what I'd almost done.'

A flicker of understanding darted through her. 'Is that why you were so angry afterwards?'

'Yeah,' he drawled, his face set in hard, angular lines.

'I blamed myself for what happened between us. If I'd been experienced I would have known that my actions were offering encouragement where it was not intended, and I would also have known not to let the situation develop as far as it did.'

'I know, honey, and it wasn't necessary for you to explain.'

He raised her hands to his lips to kiss each finger in turn, and Sarika closed her eyes for a moment to gather her scattered wits about her. It was then that a frightening little thought leapt into her mind. 'What—What else did Ayah tell you about me?'

'There are certain things that only you can tell me.' Sean released her hands to tilt her face up to his, and the brilliant blaze of his eyes held hers captive. 'Do you love me, Sarika?'

She had never been a coward, but she was shrinking inwardly from the truth when Ayah's words intruded on her thoughts. *You are living behind the closed doors of your heart because you are afraid.* Sean was waiting for her answer with a tormented look on his rugged face, and she knew she could not withhold the truth.

'Yes,' she whispered in a choked voice, and that one word seemed to ease a fraction of the tension out of his face.

'Will you marry me?'

'Yes,' she whispered this time with less difficulty, and that singing joy was exploding inside her once again as he flung her book aside and pulled her into his arms with a muttered exclamation on his lips.

He held her so tightly with her face pressed against his shoulder that she could scarcely breathe, but she did not mind, and she clung to him a little wildly in return. She had longed for the strength of his arms about her during that long night on that wretched island, and now that he was holding her she was going to revel in that secure, safe feeling growing inside her.

She turned her head slightly so that she could press

her lips to his warm throat, but he eased her out of his arms and tilted her face so that he could look into her clear eyes. 'Tell me you love me so that I can hear it and believe it.'

It's for you to open the doors of your heart and to let the truth spill from your lips, Ayah's wise words hammered at her mind, and Sarika felt a warmth slide through her body to melt that last fragment of ice about her heart.

'I . . . love you.' The words Sean had sought came haltingly from her trembling lips, and they were repeated almost immediately with more conviction as she went back into his arms and buried her face against his chest. 'Oh, Sean, I love you so much!'

'Thank God for that!' he groaned, then he was raining fiery little kisses on her face until his mouth found hers with a white-hot passion that left her limp and trembling in his arms when at last he released her lips to seek out the sensitive cord of her throat. 'I should have known the moment we met that I'd met my fate.'

'When did you know that—that you loved me?'

'I knew that afternoon when we sat in the gardens at the Taj Mahal,' he confessed, and it felt to Sarika as if her heart would burst with happiness.

'Oh, Sean, I knew it and felt it then as well, but you were so aloof and unapproachable afterwards that I was afraid you might have guessed how I felt.' Her eyes clouded with the memory of the agony she had suffered. 'I was convinced I never stood a chance that night when you said you'd sworn never to get involved with a—a virgin.'

'Darling girl, can you imagine how a confirmed bachelor must feel when he realises his bachelor days are numbered?' he smiled down at her with a hint of self-mockery in his eyes. 'I was so shaken by the discovery that I loved you that I needed time to sort myself out. I told myself that if I took you to bed once or twice I'd get you out of my system, but the discovery that you're untouched blasted that fragile hope of mine sky-high. I was mad at you, but I was even more furious with myself.'

'Why were you furious with yourself?' she asked curiously, tracing the strong curve of his jaw with her fingertips, and he caught her hand to plant a tingling kiss in her palm.

'I had some pretty nasty preconceived notions about you before we met, but you proved me wrong about each one of them, and that should have warned me that your innocence wasn't an act.' His features darkened with a mixture of anger and torment. 'God, Sarika, I never want to go through another night like the one when the *Sea Nymph* was caught in the storm!'

She had only to look at him to know what he had suffered, but that old wariness persisted. 'Are you very sure it's me you want?'

'Would you like me to prove how sure I am?' A devilish gleam lit his eyes as he undid the small bow that held her bed jacket together, and her efforts to stop him were futile.

'Be serious, Sean,' she pleaded huskily when his mouth burned its way across the shoulder he had bared to ignite little fires inside her.

'I *am* serious,' he warned, the tone and timbre of his voice exciting her as he slid a hand beneath the lace at her breast.

His mouth shifted over hers, coaxing and demanding a response she could not withhold, and the sensual, probing caress of his fingers sent an intoxicating flame darting through her body. His mouth deserted hers to roam down to her breast, nibbling and tasting her burning skin until the tantalising arousal of his tongue brought a moan of pleasure to her lips. Her eyelids fluttered down as her head fell back against the pillows, and she locked her fingers in the hair at the nape of his strong neck, encouraging him almost to continue this erotic arousal which sent arrows of desire darting along her quivering body. She pushed her hands into his shirt, seeking and finding the hard, damp warmth of his wide shoulders and his back in a fluttering caress that made him ease himself away from her with a shuddering groan.

'I guess I'd better behave myself, or I might just make love to you here and now, and that would shock Ayah out of her mourning habit,' he murmured thickly, desire still burning in his eyes when he lifted her bed jacket on to her shoulder and sat up.

Sarika giggled, her mind conjuring up Ayah's shocked expression, but the next instant she sobered. 'What are we going to do about Ayah?'

She had barely spoken those words when the door opened and Ayah walked into the room with a glass of milk which she placed on the bedside cupboard. Her glance went from Sarika's flushed face to Sean and back, then she asked suspiciously. 'Is there something happening that I don't know about?'

Sarika's cheeks felt as if they were burning with renewed fever, and she was still struggling to compose herself when Sean turned to Ayah and said: 'Sarika has agreed to marry me.'

'Oh, I am so happy for both of you!' Ayah announced excitedly, embracing them with a film of tears in her eyes before she stood back to smile down at them.

'But, Ayah,' protested Sarika anxiously, 'what will you do?'

'Do?' Ayah looked at her with some surprise. 'I will stay here, of course, and look after this house so that everything will be as you want it when you come for a visit, and I will travel to wherever you are when you need my help with your babies.'

Sean's mocking glance rested on Sarika's face, and she went red to the roots of her hair as he laughingly admonished Ayah. 'You're making Sarika blush, talking about babies when she's still trying to get used to the thought of having to share my bed!'

Ayah's laughter mingled with Sean's, and Sarika

surveyed them with a rebuke in her sparkling eyes. 'I think you're both horrible to make fun of me.'

Ayah was the first to sober, and her features suddenly adopted a stern look. 'Drink your milk, Sarika, and take your tablets.'

'Yes, Ayah,' Sarika answered meekly, but Ayah was already turning to Sean.

'And I give you no more than fifteen minutes, Sean, then you must be out of here. It is not good for Sarika at the moment to still be awake at this hour.'

'Yes, Ayah,' he mimicked Sarika's reply teasingly, and Ayah left the room with an indignant snort on her lips which changed to a contented smile when she reached the door.

Sean's expression sobered when he looked at Sarika. 'Do you trust me, honey?'

A tremulous smile curved her mouth as she raised a hand to caress his rugged cheek, and her eyes no longer hid the feelings that were pulsating through her. 'I trust you.'

He leaned over her, and in between tantalising little kisses he said: 'You'll have to marry me soon.'

'Soon,' she agreed, her heart hammering wildly in her breast.

'I'm leaving for the States in three weeks, and I want to take you with me,' he murmured, teasing the corner of her mouth with the sensual caress of his tongue. 'Shall we make it a honeymoon trip?'

'Yes,' she whispered against his lips.

'Will you always agree to everything I say?'

'Yes,' she breathed, eagerly seeking his evasive, tantalising mouth with her own.

'Liar!' Sean laughed shortly, drawing her fully into his arms and setting his hard mouth on hers at last in a tender, passionate kiss that made her senses soar.

More than fifteen minutes had elapsed before he reluctantly left her room, but his presence seemed to linger with her long afterwards, and she went to sleep that night with a smile on her lips. The fragrant perfume of the jasmine floated in through her open window, and with it came the promise of many tomorrows.

Coming Next Month in Harlequin Romances!

2743 CARTIER'S STRIKE Jane Corrie
A Sydney reporter regrets being assigned to cover the oil strike where Sean Cartier is in charge. He dislikes the press generally, and in her case, his feelings run to the extreme.

2744 QUIET LIGHTNING Tracy Hughes
Thanks to a notorious New Orleans radio-talk-show host, her parents have split up. But instead of confronting the cigar-chomping obnoxious man responsible, she encounters a charming blond god.

2745 NIGHT OF THE BEGUINE Roumelia Lane
A shop assistant on holiday falls in love with the man who shows her the beauty of Martinique—the same man her brother expects her to set up for an exclusive interview.

2746 A LAKE IN KYOTO Marjorie Lewty
Doubt enters the mind of a bride-to-be when her fiancé's ex-wife informs her of how adept the man in question can be at wriggling out of things at the last minute.

2747 VALLEY OF THE SNOWS Jean S. MacLeod
Love comes swiftly to an English secretary working in Switzerland—and so does heartache when she meets someone with prior claim to the man she loves.

2748 COME NEXT SUMMER Leigh Michaels
Circumstances force a student to share the only available apartment on campus with a political-science lecturer. Is he ruled by his heart or his head when it comes to the politics of love?

EYE OF THE STORM